Curtis Ray

Sick World

Dr Snow,

Pleasure meeting you!

HBC4

Sick World

A Story of Modern Day Slavery

A Novel

By

Dr. Mark A. Snow

Library of Congress Control Number:		2014907190
ISBN:	Hardcover	978-1-4990-0463-2
	Softcover	978-1-4990-0464-9
	eBook	978-1-4990-0462-5

Rev. date: 04/15/2014

To order additional copies of this book, contact:
Xlibris LLC
1-888-795-4274
www.Xlibris.com
Orders@Xlibris.com
619959

**Too often people will ignore fact, simply because
it was first presented as fiction.**

CHAPTER 1

ERIC DUNN WAS nobody of any consequence, at least not until the birth of his son. He lived a quiet, mundane life with his wife Sarah and there was seldom any variation in his daily, weekly, or even annual routines. He felt comfortable with that. He didn't understand how some people could stand the turmoil that came with attempting to change things. Ever since he was a child he liked knowing what each day's schedule would be. He would get up at the same time each day, go through the same activities that he did each Tuesday, if it was Tuesday, or each Saturday, if it were Saturday. Whatever day of the week it was, he had a routine for that day. Eric was raised by parents who were staunch government supporters and had no place in their life for anyone who spoke ill of the government. Eric was not political; he just wanted to live his life and let things of government take care of themselves. I guess that you could say that Eric knew his circle of influence was small, and wanted to keep it that way. Eric chose his profession, computer programming, because he knew that he could maintain the control over his life that he wanted. He never dated growing up because that was too unpredictable. He only went out once after he graduated from college simply because his employer had lined him up, and he felt that it would do his career well. His wife Sarah was attracted to Eric's pragmatic look at life, and pursued Eric after that first date. Sarah had even convinced Eric that marriage was the safest direction to go with their relationship as that would be the only way to have a regular routine. As anal as Eric was, and as much as he tried to avoid emotions, Eric thought that he might love Laura. They were very happy, and Sarah had convinced Eric to try to have a child.

As wrong as it sounds, worry was the predominant emotion that Eric felt as he watched his wife giving birth to their first child, a son that they named Eric Dunn Jr. This was a first for Eric. He had never felt this emotion, nor any real emotion, at least not since he was diagnosed with an anxiety disorder at the age of twelve. He wasn't even sure that what he was feeling was worry. But, his heart was racing, he felt a bit clammy, and his stomach tickled inside. His wife's pregnancy had gone smoothly with no complications. Each of her examinations had been unremarkable; the ultrasounds showed nothing out of the ordinary, just a healthy, well developing male fetus. She had started labor spontaneously two days past her due date, and was now in the final stages of labor. Everything had gone perfectly. So why then was he so full of worry? Perhaps it was the uncertainty of how this was going to effect his daily routine. Or could it be the cryptic message he received on a small card that was secretly slipped into his hand? An elderly nurse passed it to him as he walked out of the elevator on the fourth floor of the Barack Obama Federal Medical Center in Salt Lake City, Utah. The message read, "There is still time to save your baby", followed by a phone number. Eric knew the statistics. His son, as healthy as he may be at birth, had a 1 in 4 chance that he would not survive past his second birthday. He also had a 1 in 3 chance that he would have, or develop some type of neuro-developmental disorder before his fifth birthday. Eric wondered why there was such a horrible mortality rate among young children with all of the medical advances that they had. There were virtually no childhood diseases due to the mandatory vaccinations that each person received beginning at birth. There was no chance of an epidemic should one of these diseases have an outbreak. With the biostrip that each person had implanted at birth, they could be monitored twenty four hours of every day. If they didn't receive a mandatory vaccination, the CDC would know it. If their temperature went above 93.3 degrees Fahrenheit, the CDC would know it. If you tried to travel with an elevated temperature the TSA would know it. This would trigger a mandatory lock down of that individual until the situation was taken care of. The modern day diagnostic equipment was very advanced. Again, with just a scan of the biostrip they could see complete blood counts, heart rate, respiration, they could even get a reading on liver enzymes and kidney function. You name it, and some Government Agency could read it. Then when the International Currency Credits (ICC) were created, they linked that to the biostrip. Now it was not necessary to carry any identification or credit cards that could be lost or stolen. Anything that was purchased was paid for by a scan of the biostrip. Eric remembered as a child hearing his grandmother always warning his parents that all of the medicines and vaccines his parents gave him would some day kill him. "We are just doing what the medical experts advise." His mother would say. "Besides, it's the law." His father would add. Eric's parents were "follow the law" type of people. They always taught Eric that the government was there to help us, and they wouldn't make a law that wasn't good for the people. When Eric was 10-years-old, he got really sick after his bi-annual vaccine boosters. He remembers feeling very afraid all of the time after that. Then at age twelve, when he went in for his shots, the doctor put him on an anti-anxiety medicine. Things got alot easier after that, or at least they felt easier. Eric just coasted through life and did what he was told. He didn't see any reason to rock the boat. Now here he was in this situation, feeling things that he had not felt for a longtime. But this was different. This was not about Eric, it was about his soon to be born son. As Eric watched his wife struggle to bring this little life into the world, he noticed the preparations being made by the nurses. There were four syringes being prepared with the necessary vaccines contained in nine different bottles. *Quite a cocktail*, he thought to himself. He was then jarred out of his deep thought by one of the nurses asking him, "Mr. Dunn, you look worried, are you okay?" Then he remembered, in the rush out of the house to bring his wife to the hospital, he had forgotten all of his medications, which included his anti anxiety medication. He and his wife were so focused on the arrival of their baby boy. They had waited for five years before their name was finally drawn in the lottery giving them permission to have a child. Then it took another six months to finally conceive. The doctors assured them that Laura was fertile, and Eric had adequate sperm. They could not find a medical reason for their difficulty conceiving. The doctors suggested the use of a government-assigned surrogate. Luckily they conceived on their own without having to resort to that. "No", he answered, "I totally forgot to take my medication this morning." The nurse gave a slight vacant grin, "It happens all of the time. Go to the nurse's station down the hall, they will scan you and give you your meds. Your baby won't be here for at least another fifteen minutes." Eric could feel an anxiety in the nurse even though she seemed calm. He wasn't sure why he felt that, but he just said thank you and left the room. As Eric left the delivery room and walked down the hallway he felt uneasiness with the brightness of the lights in the hallway. He couldn't help but feel that he was somehow exposed. He also thought how convenient it was that they would be able to scan his biostrip and know what medications to give him. They would also be able to deduct the ICC to pay for them. On his way to the nurse's station, he noticed a young couple a few doors down from his wife's room, holding a small bundle in their arms, crying hysterically. He could overhear the doctor telling them of the unfortunate passing of their baby who was just thirty-six hours old. He thought of the card in his pocket. He walked right passed the nurse's station, and went out into a common waiting area. He found a corner that seemed to have a little less light, reached into his pocket, took out the card and dialed the number on his cell phone. After two rings, a woman's voice said, "What room number?"

"What?" Eric replied.

"What room number is your baby being delivered in?" the woman asked again.

"406," Eric replied.

The phone went silent. Eric put his phone away and rushed back to his wife's room. As he entered, everything was as he had left it. He felt much more comfortable in the softened light of the delivery room. The tall, red-headed, slender nurse that had sent him to the nurse's station gave another forced grin at him and asked how he was feeling.

"Much better" he lied.

He could tell that she did not believe him. Just then, an older nurse came into the room, she was the nurse that gave him the card. She was shorter than the other nurse and from the number of pins and other insignia on her uniform coupled with the slight graying of her dark hair was obviously more experienced and the younger nurse's superior. She didn't even look his way, but went right over to the tall red-headed nurse and whispered something to her. They smiled at each other, and the red headed nurse left the room. Eric's heart began pounding even harder in his chest, and he could now feel beads of sweat forming on his forehead.

As Eric stood looking through the glass into the nursery where his newborn sonlie, he tried to calm himself so as not to bring attention to the fact that he had not taken his medication. He felt that same feeling of vulnerability that he had experienced before when walking down the bright hallway. His focus shifted from his son to his own reflection in the window. He was average height for his day, about 5 feet 6 inches. He had a very slender build and stood with his shoulders slightly rolled forward and his head cocked off to the right a bit. *At least I still have a full head of hair*, he thought to himself. Eric was an average looking fellow despite the obvious posture problems which were probably due to staring at a computer all day, every day.

Eric worked for a large computer software company in Hyland, Utah. One thing stood out as he looked at himself in the reflection, and that was that his tick had stopped, or at least slowed tremendously. Normally he had a quick, uncontrollable head jerk to the left every sixty to ninety seconds. He didn't really think much of it usually as he had just learned to live with it, but now he could not help but notice its absence. He had never felt anything like this in his entire life. He felt overwhelming joy when he thought of his new son, and excitement to hold him and play with him. That feeling would then be replaced by anxiety over the strange events during his birth, and the unmistakable feeling that he was under observation. Up and down his feelings went, and it took all he had to hold it together.

"Would you like a cup of tea?" a soft female voice said from behind him. He turned to find the elderly nurse that had entered the delivery room after his weird telephone call. "You look terrible" she said. "We better get you calmed down before somebody notices." Eric could feel her strength and calm demeanor. He just followed her in silence as they made their way to the cafeteria. She filled two cups, one with hot water and another with cold water. She then took him to a table in the back away from anyone else. She placed what appeared to be a tea bag in the hot water, then handed him a couple of large pills.

"Here, take these."

"What are they?" he asked.

"They won't hurt you, they are just some herbal pills to help calm your nerves, and make you feel more comfortable. The lights will stop bothering you. Just take them."

Eric didn't know how she knew that the lights were bothering him, but he could tell, somehow, that he could trust her. He put them in his mouth and washed them down with water. They left somewhat of an earthy taste in his mouth. As he brought his head forward from drinking the water, his eyes caught a small tattoo, actually two small tattoos on her right wrist, just two small dots about a quarter of an inch apart from each other.

"I'm sorry to have to have been so mysterious today, but you have to know two things. First, know that you have, for probably the first time in your life, made a correct decision regarding health, both of yours and your baby's. Second, know that what you have decided to do is against the law, extremely risky, and could cost you your life. It may even cause you to lose your family. So before we go any further, I need to know if you wish to continue."

Eric looked at her in silence for what seemed like a few minutes, but was probably just a few seconds. How could he make a decision with so much information lacking? He didn't know who she was, nor did he know that what she said about his "good decision" was true. Although he didn't doubt what she had said about losing his family, if his wife found out. But then again, what had he done? He made a phone call, and gave a strange woman on the other end of the telephone a room number. It dawned on him that this is why she was asking him this now, because he was about to learn more and that would make him vulnerable. Eric looked passed her and noticed a couple of men in dark suits and ties sitting across the room staring blankly at Eric and this lady. One of the men was wearing sunglasses.

"Are they with you?" Eric asked. She didn't even look, but the kind smile left her face and she said, "No. They are not." Eric felt her anxiety."

Are they wearing sunglasses?"

"Yes," Eric replied, "One of them is."

"I need to hurry", she said. Do you want to continue?" she asked again.

Eric looked into her kind gray-blue eyes that seemed so clear and present. Her expression was so unlike the vague vacant look that he was used to seeing in almost everybody else, including one of the two men that was watching them.

"Do I want to continue with what?" Eric asked. "I don't even know what I have done other than making a phone call."

The nurse stared deep into Eric's eyes, "That phone call prevented your baby from possibly being killed by the poisons that they were going to inject into him. Now, do you wish to continue?"

"Again, do I want to continue with what?" Eric said firmly.

"Are you asking me if I wish to continue breaking the law by not having my son vaccinated? If so, I don't even think that that is possible. You and I both know that by tomorrow night he will have a biostrip implanted in his arm, and they will know what vaccines he has and has not had." I am not even sure that the vaccinations are bad for him. Why would they give us vaccinations that were bad for us?"

The woman listened attentively, then she calmly said, "Eric, I do not have the time here to educate you completely on the truth about vaccinations, but if you will simply, for a moment, connect the dots. Look at how the rates of neuro-developmental disorders in children have risen in the last twenty years. Look at how the numbers of vaccinations have also risen in the last twenty years. Ask yourself who benefits financially from all of that?"

"Not the government," Eric said.

"No, the governments are pawns used to enforce the rules that make those who are really in power wealthier."

"What if I say that I don't want to continue?" asked Eric.

She calmly said, "Then I would walk away, and you would never see me again."

Eric noticed some emotion in her voice, and thought that he saw her eyes becoming moist.

"You must think about this Eric. What do I have to gain from you not vaccinating your son?"

"Nothing," said Eric.

"That's right. The only reason that I would like to help you prevent from having to vaccinate your son is to save your son."

"I don't want to lose my family," Eric said.

"If you do exactly what we tell you, then you will be okay. This isn't the first child that we have saved."

Eric asked, "Who's we?"

She smiled, "I am not alone Eric, and neither will you be."

Eric sat quietly for a moment. He looked over her shoulder at the two men staring at them, then back at the woman.

"I am not sure why, but my gut tells me that you are right and that I should listen to you."

"Good" she said. "Tomorrow you will be told by your doctor that your son is doing well, but that he has a case of jaundice, nothing too severe, and not to be alarmed. He will tell you that they will be releasing your wife and son to go home, but that you will be taking a light therapy lamp home with you to help with his jaundice. They will have you scan his biostrip daily so that they can monitor his bilirubin levels."

"How do you know that my son has jaundice?" Eric asked.

"He doesn't," she replied.

"Then why will the doctor tell me that he does?"

"Because if he has nothing wrong with him, they will suspect that he didn't receive his vaccinations. I have to go now. How do you feel?" she asked.

Eric had been sipping his tea through out their conversation, and hadn't even realized how calm he was feeling. His heart wasn't racing, nor did he feel clammy anymore. But he had clarity of thought that he couldn't remember ever having.

"I feel really good Clare," he said looking at her name tag.

"What did you give me?"

"Just some herbs to help calm you, and clear your head. You may hear from me again, but if not, you will know who you can trust by the mark."

"What mark?" he queried.

She pointed to the two dots on her wrist as she said, "Connect the dots, Eric. One more thing, those men will probably come over and ask you questions. It is important that you remain calm while answering them. The herbs that I gave you will help. They have a way of detecting your emotions, and they will know you are lying if you do not control your emotions. Try to think of other things when you answer their questions, things like your family or work. Things that won't cause your heart beat to increase."

Then she stood up, shook his hand in a very business-like manner and walked out of the room. The two men watched her as she walked out, and then turned back to look at Eric. He tried to look casual and found it easier to do now that he was so calm. The two men that had been watching them stood up and walked toward Eric.

"Mr. Dunn?" A short slender, mature looking man with fully gray hair asked.

"Yes." Eric replied.

"Mr. Dunn, I am Dr. Bernstien, Head of the Neonatal Department of Vaccines and Disease Prevention here at the hospital, and this, pointing to the man in the sunglasses, is Dr. Calvin of the Centers for Disease Control. Has anyone in the hospital approached you about not giving your son his mandatory vaccinations?"

"No," Eric lied, and quickly thought of his wife and son so as to not show any emotion as he lied. "Why?"

Dr. Calvin looked at Dr Bernstein and nodded.

"What were you discussing with Miss Homer?"

"Who is Miss Homer?" asked Eric.

"She is the head nurse from Labor and Delivery that you were just talking to."

"Oh, Clare? She was just giving me some advice since I am a first-time father. You know, telling me how I can help my wife with diaper changing and feedings and such. I think that she saw the deer in the headlights look in my eyes and was just trying to comfort me." Eric laid out this lie with ease, owing to the fact that he had anticipated their question. The two doctors both looked at each other. Dr. Calvin nodded.

Dr Bernstein turned to Eric and said, "Sorry to bother you Mr. Dunn, but Home Land Security has contacted us about a possible terrorist threat. They have reports that someone, whether acting alone or as a group, is attempting to stop people from getting their babies vaccinated. As you should know Mr. Dunn, this is considered an act of bio-terrorism. Homeland Security is sending a counter terrorism team out to investigate. If you or your wife is contacted, it is critical that you let us know. We don't want your son to have to be raised by someone else while you rot in prison."

Eric was silent.

"Congratulations on your new son."

"Thank you," Eric said, quickly thinking of something at work, as he stood up.

"I better get back to my wife now before she thinks that I deserted her."

As Eric walked back to the room where his wife was recovering, his head was spinning. *What am I doing?*, He thought to himself. *This is crazy! I can't get away with this.* Eric was always suspicious of the vaccines, and nobody really agreed with them being made mandatory. President Obama had rammed his healthcare bill through the Senate and after signing the "Anti-free speech" Bill into law, and with the help of the Homeland Security Act and International treaties that dealt with environmental issues, he was able to ram through other legislation that the majority of the American people did not agree with, like the mandatory vaccinations.

Eric entered his wife's room. She was sleeping peacefully. Eric gave her a kiss on her forehead, which caused her to stir.

"I want our baby," she said quietly.

"I will get the nurse," Eric said. He pushed the call button for the nurse.

"May I help you?" A nurse on the other end asked.

"We would like to have our baby with us please."

"I will have someone from the nursery bring him down."

A few minutes later, the nurse knocked on the door and then entered the room pushing a little clear plastic bassinet on a metal stand.

"Here is your baby" she said. "He has been sleeping right through all of the other baby's crying. If he doesn't wake up in the next thirty minutes, you might want to wake him to feed him."

"Are you breast feeding or bottle feeding?"

"Breast feeding" Mrs. Dunn replied.

"I will have one of the nurses come by with some information for you, and to answer any questions that you may have regarding breast feeding."

The nurse left the room. As Eric looked down at his newborn son cradled in the arms of his sweet wife, he was overwhelmed with gratitude. He could feel his face flush and tears welling up in his eyes. Again, he was feeling more emotion than he remembers ever feeling before.

"He's perfect," his wife said as she turned her head up to look at Eric.

"Why are you crying?"

"I'm just overwhelmed with gratitude right now."

"There was a couple just two doors down that lost their baby just a day after it was born. Probably those damn vaccinations that they force us to give them."

His wife rolled her eyes, "I doubt that honey. The vaccinations are safe. The government wouldn't give them if they weren't."

Eric's heart dropped. His wife's response had told him clearly where she stood on the matter, and now he was afraid to tell her what he had done. Now what was he going to do? Just then, there was a knock on the door, and another nurse came in.

"I understand that you will be breast feeding your baby," she said.

"Uh huh . . ."

"Well, I have a few pamphlets for you, and I can help you get started with that if you like." The nurse handed the pamphlets to Eric and then went to work helping his wife Sarah. Eric stepped back to the other side of the room to be out of the way, and sat down. He began thumbing through the pamphlets; *Breast pumps and how to use them, Storing your milk for your baby, How will you know that you are producing enough milk?* . . . Eric's jaw dropped as he read the title of the last pamphlet: *Why the government wants you to vaccinate your baby.*

He looked up at the nurse who was helping his wife, and noticed a couple of small dots on the underside of her wrist. She looked over at him and smiled. Eric took that pamphlet and put it in his pocket. He wanted to read it, but did not want his wife to see it.

Things were quiet, Sarah was asleep and so was Eric, Jr. Eric sat back in the rocking chair and pulled out the pamphlet that the nurse had given him. He placed it inside one of the other pamphlets to disguise it, should his wife wake up. The pamphlet gave a history that he had never heard.

In 1918, six of the wealthiest people in the world held a secret meeting on Buck Island just off the coast of Tortola. The purpose of this meeting was to brainstorm a way for them to ensure uninterrupted expansion of their wealth and power. They determined that they needed to control a product that would be used by everyone worldwide. They determined that the product that they would need to control would be Healthcare.

Once they decided on a product, they had to design a way to create the demand. They needed to get as many people as possible to need their product. In order to need their product, people needed to be sick. They decided that if they could get as many people as possible to take one medicine, just one, this could be the "baited hook" that would reel them in and make them life long customers. So what was that one? A vaccine.

They knew that there was a great deal of fear of certain illnesses that had caused many deaths. Creating vaccinations for these illnesses and promoting them as a way to eradicate the illness from mankind would unite people to their cause. This would then lead to governments passing laws to make their vaccines mandatory. They knew that the vaccinations would injure some people, and this would lead to chronic, non-life threatening illnesses that would require lifelong medical management. If they could increase the number of vaccinations needed, they could make more people chronically ill, and in need of more healthcare.

It was genius. They would own the pharmaceutical companies that would make the vaccines. They would own the pharmaceutical companies that would make the medicines to treat the illnesses caused by the vaccines. They would start non-profit research foundations to find a "cure" for the illnesses caused by their vaccines. They would develop treatments requiring expensive devices that they would manufacture and sell. They would fund medical schools to train medical doctors to sell their product. They would own insurance companies that would charge high premiums and pay out little in comparison for their product. Thereby making people pay out of pocket for their product, and that part that the insurance did pay is really just moving their own money from one part of their organization to another. They would finance political parties and candidates on both sides of the aisle to ensure legislation that would force people to use their products.

The plan was laid, and put into action.

Eric found out that since the plan was put into action, it had grown. Now, according to the pamphlet there are extremely wealthy and powerful people that sit on elite committees to make critical decisions in regards to public policy. These decisions are made to set the government in motion making laws and policies that benefit this elite group. This group has the majority ownership in pharmaceutical companies, medical schools, insurance companies, automobile manufacturers, and petroleum companies. The pamphlet called the Elite group the Insiders. He read of how the Insiders had created a way for them to always have plenty of customers. They used powerful lobbying and made big donations to political campaigns, which gave them some sway on the votes cast by those that they backed. In this way, they were able to get legislation passed that required everyone to have health insurance. Most people are not aware of the fact that the Insiders also own the insurance companies. They were able to get legislation requiring vaccinations of everyone. The pharmaceutical companies are also owned by the Insiders. The vaccinations would cause side effects ranging from death to neuro-developmental disorders, to chronic auto-immune diseases like Rheumatoid Arthritis, Lupus, Type I Diabetes Miletus, Asthma, ADHD, etc. The Insiders were not after the deaths, but they were after the chronic conditions. This would guarantee future patients for them. It would also allow them to set up research foundations to "find a cure" that would bring in huge amounts of tax free money. Owning the medical schools would allow them to control the education that the doctors received, thus controlling the practice of medicine to benefit their interests. As he read, he developed a pit in his stomach, and a rage built up inside him.

"What are you reading?" Sarah asked, startling Eric.

"Oh, just this pamphlet on breast feeding," he replied.

Sarah chuckled, "Those are for me to read, you dummy. Let me see it."

Eric hadn't anticipated his wife asking him to hand her the pamphlet. Now how was he going to prevent her from seeing what he was really reading? He stood up to hand her the pamphlet, and as he did he faked a fumble and dropped both of the pamphlets under her bed.

"Clumsy!" she laughed. Eric bent down and picked up the Breast Feeding Pamphlet, but could not see the other pamphlet that he had been reading. He handed her the breast feeding pamphlet and sat down. As he sat there, he discretely but earnestly searched the floor for the other pamphlet.

At a little after 9 P.M., the nurse from the nursery came in.

"Mrs. Dunn, I'm going to take your baby back to the nursery for a little while so you can get some rest. We will bring him back in a couple of hours. Mr. Dunn, you should go home and get some rest also. It is nearly 10 P.M.. You can come back at about 9 A.M. tomorrow morning."

Eric agreed, and the nurse pulled the baby bassinet on wheels back out of the room. As she did, Eric noticed the lost pamphlet on the floor beneath where the bassinet had been. He quickly put his foot on it to hide it, and spoke to his wife.

"Are you going to be ok if I go home?"

"Yes, I'm just going to sleep. You go home and get some rest."

Eric kissed his wife goodbye, bent down and pretended to tie his shoe, picking up the pamphlet. He said goodnight, left the room and walked to the elevators. He folded up the pamphlet and placed it in his back pocket. Whatever herbs Clare had given him must had worn off, because he was feeling that anxiety again, and he was bothered by the bright lights in the halls and the elevator. As he entered the elevator, a small Hispanic lady dressed in housekeeping attire bumped into him as she rushed past him to exit the elevator. "Excuse me, Sir," she said as she hurried on her way. Eric entered the elevator and started down to the parking garage. As he was riding the elevator down, he suddenly felt flushed and he broke out into a cold sweat. He could hardly wait for the elevator to open so that he could get some fresh air. The dim lights of the parking garage were a welcome relief, but he couldn't shake the feeling that he was being watched. When Eric got to his car, he reached into his pocket for his keys and felt his cell phone in there. "That's odd" he thought to himself, "I usually keep my cell phone in the right pocket." As he thought that he placed his right hand on his right pocket, and felt a cell phone there also. Eric pulled the cell phone out of his right pocket and instantly recognized it as his own. Puzzled he looked around, while reaching into his other pocket for the other cell phone. He noticed security cameras on the walls of the parking garage, and decided to leave the other cell phone in his pocket for now. He pulled out his keys and got into his car and drove away. A few blocks away from the hospital the phone in his left pocket began to ring. He pulled it out and answered it.

"Hello?"

"Mr. Dunn?", a man's voice asked.

"Yes" said Eric.

"Mr. Dunn, you don't know me but I have to speak with you."

"Who are you?" asked Eric, "And how did I get this cell phone?"

"It was dropped into your pocket inside the hospital."

Eric thought back to the Hispanic lady that bumped into him.

"Mr. Dunn, Clare asked me to contact you. There is a grocery store on your way home. It is on the corner of Franklin and Harvard. Stop there and go to the dairy section. You will buy a gallon of skim milk. Look for the gallon with the blue lid and a couple of small black dots on the bottom of the jug. They will look like the mark on Clare's wrist. Please look inside the gallon of milk for information that you need. Please dispose of this cell phone after this call. Be sure to completely destroy the memory card, and wipe the phone clean of your finger prints. Goodbye."

The phone went silent.

Eric pulled into the grocery store parking lot and sat in his car for a few minutes trying to grasp all that had been going on. He was starting to feel physically ill. His whole body was aching, and he felt feverish. *Just what I need right now,* he thought to himself. *Maybe I've gotten in over my head. If I have a fever, I won't even make it into the store. The bioscanners will pick it up and I will be locked down. What if I just chuck the phone, and don't get the milk? Then what?* As he thought of this, his mind flashed back to that other couple in the hospital holding the lifeless body of their new baby in their arms. *No,* he thought. *I have to do this for my son.*

Eric opened up the back of the cell phone that he had received the call on, and removed the memory card. He broke the memory card in half, then took out a handkerchief and wiped down the outside of the cell phone. He got out of the car and walked toward the store entrance. As he entered the store, he dropped the cell phone into the outside garbage can. He dropped one half of the memory card into a trash can just inside the door, and held onto the other half of the memory card. He was bothered by the bright lights in the store, and he couldn't wait to get out of there. He had never been bothered by lights before, and figured that it was just because he was sick. He went straight to the pharmacy and picked up a box of Tylenol Cold and Flu. Then he went to the dairy section. He found the case holding the skim milk with blue lids. He scanned the bottoms of the jugs and near the middle of the case he spotted a jug that had two small dots on it. Eric picked it up, went to the check out stand and swiped his wrist to pay for the milk and Tylenol.

CHAPTER 2

S ARAH STIRRED AWAKE at about 11:15 P.M. She was in quite a bit of pain. As she rolled over, she noticed someone walking out of her room and shutting the door. "Nurse?" she called. There was no response. Sarah was shocked by the pain that she felt, she pushed the call button.

"Can I help you?" a voice asked over the speaker.

"Can I get something for pain please? And I think that it is time to feed my baby."

"I'll be in after my rounds," the nurse replied with a slightly irritated tone in her voice as though Sarah was an inconvenience.

Sarah waited for what seemed to be thirty minutes or more, while her pain increased in intensity. Finally, the nurse came in her room with some Tylenol.

"Were you in here checking on me a bit ago?" Sarah asked.

"No," replied the nurse.

"Oh well, it must have been one of the other nurses."

Sarah was shocked when the nurse told her that she had been the only nurse on the floor since the shift change at 11 P.M.. The nurse was puttering around the room checking machines and making notes. Sarah could sense that the nurse was efficient, but didn't really want to be here. She looked tired and bothered, as if her job was keeping her from something more important. Sarah wondered who it had been that she had seen leaving her room? She didn't say anything more to the nurse about it.

"Can I have my baby now?" she asked the nurse relunctary, not wanting to add more interruption to her night.

The nurse sighed, "I will check with the nursery, and bring him down to you in a few minutes." Sarah felt frustrated and upset. She felt as though the nurse was going to take her sweet time getting Eric, Jr. for her. *What does she care?*, Sarah thought to herself as she lie back in her bed and waited for the medicine to take affect. Soon she had dozed off again.

Sarah awoke with a sudden jerk, and saw another lady standing over her baby, who was in his clear plastic bassinet next to her bed. The nurse must have rolled him in when she was asleep and left him by her, not wanting to disturb her. This other woman was in a robe and slippers, her eyes were red and swollen as if she had been crying a lot. She was looking down at Eric, Jr. while softly carressing his chest. Sarah heard a sob come from her.

"Who are you?" Sarah asked softly but warily.

"I saw them kill my baby," the other lady said as she softly rubbed Eric, Jr.'s chest. Sarah's heart was in her throat in an instant. She sat up quickly and pulled her baby's bassinet to her. Reaching in, she picked Eric, Jr. up and cradled him in her arms.

"What do you mean?" Sarah asked.

The other mother sobbed some more, then replied, "My baby was pink and healthy and crying when she was born. They placed her on my belly and I felt her strength. There was nothing wrong with her. Then they put that poison in her and I watched as the life drained from her. She cried at first just like any baby would do, and then she just went limp." She paused for a moment while she sobbed, then she continued. "I called to the nurse, and they took her to the nursery right away. I laid there while they sewed me up and wondered what was going on with my little girl. I kept asking about her but they just said that they were working on her and she would be fine. Finally after I had been moved into my room, the doctor came in to talk with my husband and I. I'm sorry. he said, Your baby girl did not make it. Her lungs could not expand, and we were unable to save her. I know he was lying. I know that my little girl's lungs were perfect."

She broke out in an uncontrollable sob. Sarah sat there filled with pity and compassion for this poor broken hearted lady that she didn't even know. She did not know what to say.

"Why did they kill my baby?!" she asked sobbing.

"I'm so sorry for your loss," Sarah said with warmth, "I'm sure that they didn't kill your little girl on purpose, though. Why would they do that?"

"It's the poison that they put in her. That's what killed her." The woman said with odium in her voice. Sarah could see the change in her countenance and the rage building up inside this poor woman. She held her son tightly against her chest.

"You were lucky" she said, "Your baby survived. But you better not let them keep giving him those poisons or something will happen to him also. You need to keep your baby safe," the woman said as she broke into another sob.

Sarah got up and placed Eric in his bassinet, then lovingly put her arms around this poor grieving stranger. Just then a nurse came in the room.

"Mrs. Rasmussen! There you are. We have been worried about you," the nurse said while she reached for a small black hand held communication device on her lanyard. "I found Mrs. Rasmussen, she is in room 406," she announced on her small handheld device. This was the same nurse that Sarah had spoken to earlier. *I bet that she is really upset now,* Sarah thought to herself. *I mean, how dare this lady interrupt my game of Solitaire just because her baby died?!,* Sarah thought with sarcasm and disgust.

"Mrs. Rasmussen, you need to come back to your room. It's time for your medication." the nurse said. Mrs. Rasmussen turned from Sarah's embrace and screamed at the nurse.

"No! You are not giving me anymore of your poison!"

The nurse pushed a button on her handheld and then approached Mrs. Rasmussen. Sarah quickly pushed Eric's bassinet to the other side of the bed and stood in front of him.

"Mrs. Rasmussen, we are not giving you poison. We just want to help you stay calm so that you don't hurt yourself."

Two male nurses walked through the door just then. A mixture of fear and rage filled Mrs. Rasmussen's eyes as she screamed and tried to run through the nurse and the two men to get to the door. They easily restrained her while they gave her an injection in her arm. Within a few seconds, she was limp and calm and unable to stand on her own. The two male nurses gently helped her into a wheel chair that was waiting in the hallway.

"I'm sorry for that Mrs. Dunn" the nurse said.

"I don't know if I would take losing a child any differently than she. Can I get you anything?"

"No thank you, I'm fine." Sarah was shaking inside, and could hardly hold herself together. She was also shocked at the apparent show of sympathy from the nurse.

Eric, Jr. started to cry, and she turned to him and picked him up. As she sat in her quiet, dimly-lit room nursing her baby boy, she felt frightened and alone. She longed for her husband to come and take her home. Sarah could not get the image of that poor woman out of her mind, and that made her think of her own mother. Sarah had been raised by her Dad. She was an only child, and grew up happy and loved, yet without a mother. Shortly after her birth her parents divorced, and she never heard from or even saw her mother. She didn't even know her name. Sarah grew up in a lower middle class household. Her Dad, Ben, was not an educated man, but he had learned a trade early in life and worked in a sheet metal factory. He had been employed by the same company since graduating from high school. Sarah's dad worked long hours sometimes, and at other times he hardly worked at all. There were about three times in her life that her dad was out of work for a short period of time due to lay-offs. But Ben was very frugal, and he managed his money wisely. Therefore, Sarah never went without, nor did she ever really want for things. Sarah's Aunt Betsy, her father's older sister, was like a surrogate mother to Sarah. She was the one that helped her through those very important "girl moments" growing up, and Sarah loved her aunt Betsy very much. In her late teens, Sarah asked her Dad about her Mom again. He said that she was trying to hurt Sarah, by not getting her vaccinated.

"That poison will kill her!" she would say.

Ben was not as educated as Sarah's mom, so he had a hard time arguing with her about it. Ben was adamant though that the vaccines were a good thing, or the FDA would not approve of them. Besides, it was against the law to not vaccinate. If they didn't vaccinate Sarah, the government would revoke their parenting license and give Sarah to a government appointed family to be raised. So he divorced Sarah's mom and had her parental rights revoked. That was all he would say at the time, and he told Sarah that he didn't like to speak of it. He died before Sarah could get any more information from him. Later she tried to find out who her mother was from her birth certificate, but the government had removed her mother's name completely. Sarah didn't know any of her aunts or uncles on her mother's side. Sarah asked her aunt Betsy what she knew about her mother, but got no information other than the same response each time, "Your mother loved you very much." Betsy's dying words to Sarah were, "Your mother will be there when you need her." Sarah lied there thinking about her aunt Betsy's final words. Just then, the door to her room opened and a nurse whom she had never seen before came quickly to her bed. She had the look of an angry mother as she bent down without even looking at Sarah and took Eric, Jr. from her. She was followed by two men in suits that moved to each side of the bed to hold Sarah down. Sarah was frightened, and didn't know what was going on.

"What is this? Give me back my baby!" Sarah screamed as she tried to free herself from the two men holding her down.

"You thought we would't know Mrs. Dunn?" the nurse said with a snide grin. She laid Eric, Jr. on a table and began to unwrap him from his blanket. She removed his diaper, then laid him on his side. She then removed a handful of syringes from her pocket. "We always know!" she said. She then began to inject Eric, Jr. with whatever was in the syringes, one by one.

"No!" Sarah screamed, "That poison will kill him! That poison will kill him! That poison will kill him!"

She woke with a start. She looked quickly around the room that was now lit by the warm sunlight streaming through the window. She saw Eric, Jr. sleeping quietly in his bassinet, and there was no one else in the room. Sarah laid back with a deep sigh of relief.

"Just a dream," she whispered. *Probably because of the visit I had last night from that poor Mrs. Rasmussen. I wonder how she is doing,* Sarah thought to herself. *I will have to check in on her.* As she laid there in the quiet of her room, she rolled her head to the side to look at her son. Gradually she became aware that Eric, Jr. didn't seem to be breathing. Quickly she reached into the bassinet to pick him up, and noticed how cold and stiff his body felt. She rolled him from his side toward her, onto his back and screamed when she saw his pale, blue, lifeless face.

"Mrs. Dunn, Mrs. Dunn!"

Sarah opened her eyes to see her nurse standing by her bed.

"It's time to feed your baby again," the nurse said, and handed Sarah her warm, cuddly little boy wrapped snugly in his blanket. Sarah wept as she suckled her sweet little boy, and was grateful that she had just been dreaming.

CHAPTER 3

B Y THE TIME Eric got home he was so sick that he could barely see straight.

Eric and Laura lived in a town home type apartment that had two floors. The main floor was comprised of a small living room that you stepped down into from the entry at the front door. Straight through the living room there was a sliding glass door that opened out to a small fenced in patio area. On one side of the living room was two steps that went up to a small dining area, which was separated from the small kitchen by a counter. Through the kitchen was a laundry room that had a door out to the single car garage. Off of the main entry was a flight of stairs that went up six steps to a landing, and then another six steps coming back the other way to the upstairs floor. Upstairs there was the master bedroom to the right with its master bath. To the left was the other bedroom that they had made up into a nursery for Eric, Jr. Straight ahead from the top of the stairs was the second bathroom that included the bioscanner. This was a cylindrical plastic room, with a sliding glass door, that had a small round stool to sit on, a video phone, and a place to put your arm to have your biostrip scanned. This was how they could check up on you to see if you might be carrying a contagion. It was mandatory in all homes.

Eric went into the kitchen and took some Tylenol. Hhe sat down at the table to open his milk jug. He sat and stared at it for a while. *This is stupid*, he thought to himself. *I'm looking at this milk jug like it is a bomb. What could possibly be in here?* He examined it closely, hefted it and felt its weight. Except for the two dots, that any other person would not pay any attention to, it was just like any other gallon of milk that he had purchased in the past. He unscrewed the lid, and looked inside. *Milk*, he thought to himself. He got a gallon pitcher from the cabinet, and poured the milk out slowly, looking for anything other than milk to come out. After it was empty, he looked inside the jug expecting to see something, but there was nothing. He sat back in his chair confused. *What in the hell is it that I'm supposed to find?*, he thought. His head was pounding, his body ached and he felt very chilled. He heard the latch on his front door turn. Then a chime followed by a lady's voice, "Please enter your bio-scanner, we have detected an elevated temperature." *Great!*, Eric thought. *Now I'm going to be quarantined.*

Eric entered the bioscanner and sat down on the stool. He placed his arm in the biostrip scanning device. The video screen came on. An attractive young nurse asked him, "How are you feeling today, Mr. Dunn?"

"Actually", Eric started, "I feel like death warmed over."

There was no use in lying. They would have his temperature and all of his vitals within sixty seconds.

"We don't have any record of your fellow workers or family members being ill. There have not been any contagions found at the hospital where your son was born, the only opportunity that you have had to pick up a bug was at the grocery store where you stopped tonight, but your bioscanner is showing that your temperature had begun to rise prior to stopping there."

"I'm going to have to take a look at your blood count Mr. Dunn. It will be just a few more minutes."

As he sat there he thought about how they were able to track all of his movements. They knew exactly where he had been, and who he had been around. No wonder Clare and all of her cohorts were being so clandestine. But how would they be able to prevent his son from getting all of his required vaccines? He knew that in a very short while they would be implanting Eric, Jr.'s biostrip, and then they would be able to know what vaccines he really has received.

"Mr. Dunn", the nurse came back on, "your blood titers indicate that you have not taken your medications. This is probably the reason for your elevated temperature. You should feel better after taking your medications. I will go ahead and clear you for leaving your home. Have a nice day, Mr. Dunn, and congratulations on the birth of your new son."

The screen turned off, and again Eric felt it odd that someone whom he has never met in person, nor spoke with prior to this event, knew about and was congratulating him on his new son. As he walked out of the bioscanner, he heard the latches on his doors turn, and he knew then that he could leave. He went back down stairs to the table to look at the milk jug again. He couldn't figure out what he was missing. He thought about taking his meds so that he could feel better, but he was enjoying his clarity of thought, and even though he was sick, he felt like he was really alive for the first time in years. After sitting there for about twenty minutes, disgusted and tired, he left it all sitting on the table and went upstairs to go to bed.

After a very long miserable night of tossing and turning, Eric decided to get up and take a hot shower and get ready to go pick up Sarah and Eric, Jr. Although it was only 6 A.M., and he couldn't go into her room until 9 A.M. at the earliest, and they probably wouldn't be released until later that evening, he couldn't stand lying in bed any longer. In the middle of getting ready he remembered the gallon of milk. *There has got to be something in that jug*, he thought. Eric was in the middle of shaving when it dawned on him "The lid!" he blurted out loud. Quickly, he wiped the shaving cream off of his face and ran downstairs. He picked up the milk jug lid and examined it. He looked on the inside of the lid and didn't see anything at first. Then his eyes caught the glimps of what looked like a seam around the inside top of the lid. He hurriedly pulled a steak knife from the kitchen drawer to see if he could open the seam. With very little effort he was able to pry out a round, blue piece of plastic from the inside of the lid revealing some writing. It was an address that read2712 East Quail Covey Court, and the name Sebastian.

He had to find this place, and he had time before going to the hospital. He ran upstairs, threw on his clothes, and dashed out to his car. After entering the address in his GPS, he realized where, or at least what part of town, this address was in. It wasn't quite light yet, as the sun was behind the mountains, causing them to look like a tear across the royal blue skyline above the twinkling lights of the city. As he turned onto Quail Covey Court, he came to a large wrought iron gate just thirty feet from the corner. On each side of the gate was a nine foot high, eighteen inch thick red brick wall that went on in each direction as far as he could see. On the inside of the wall and along each side of the road on the other side of the gate he could only see tall Lodge Pole Pines. On top of the tall brick posts that held the gate up he saw cameras, and just in front of the gate to his left he saw a speaker phone. He sat there for a long time, wondering if he should push the button on the speaker phone. What would he say? If he pushed the button whoever was on the other side would ask him what he wanted. *Um, I found this address on a milk bottle cap*, would sound so dumb. It was fully light now, and out of the corner of his eye he noticed one of the cameras panning toward his direction and stopping.

"Well, they know that I'm here," he said out loud.

Eric looked at his watch, it was 8A.M.. *Here goes nothing*, he thought, and rolled his window down and pushed the button. He heard a long beep that stopped when he released the button. After a fifteen second silence, he heard a man's voice.

"May I help you?" The voice asked.

"Um, is Sebastian home?" he asked sheepishly.

After asking, he thought, *I sound like a 12 year-old asking if his friend could come out and play.* There was no response for what seemed like an eternity. Then, two armed men in uniform appeared at the side of the road on the inside of the gate, one of them holding the leash of a large Rottweiler. Then the gate began to open and the same male voice said, "Please proceed down the lane to the house. Stay on the road straight ahead, and do not turn off. He slowly began to roll forward down the lane, past the two armed guards. The large Rottweiler watched him drive by, but seemed not to care much. He didn't bark, he simply watched Eric's car as it rolled by. *I'm sure his demeanor would change in a hurry with the right command from his handler,* Eric thought to himself. *That would not be a pleasant experience.* As Eric drove down the winding lane, he passed another small lane cutting off to the right. He wondered what was down that lane, but didn't dare deviate from the one that he was on. About a mile onto the compound, the thick forest of trees cleared and the road opened to a large circular driveway with a beautiful fountain set in the middle of it. It sat in front of a huge colonial style mansion with six white pillars in front. On either side was a beautifully manicured lawn with trimmed hedges and colorful flower beds. Eric pulled his car around to the front door. Almost as soon as he put his car in park there was a man opening his door for him.

"Good morning, Mr. Dunn," the well dressed gentleman said. "Please come with me."

"Who are you?" asked Eric.

"I am just the Steward of the estate. My name is James."

"Who do you work for?" Eric was a little hesitant to leave his car without more information.

"I work for the master of the estate, of course. Please follow me."

Eric didn't get the information that he had requested, but he didn't want to push too hard. He wanted to know who he was there to meet, and was afraid that if he pushed too hard, he would be asked to leave.

CHAPTER 4

IN A SMALL two bedroom apartment in Washington D.C., a telephone rang. It took two rings to stir Allen Cranfield out of a sound sleep.

"Hello!" he said, trying to sound alert. "Yes, this is he . . ." Salt Lake City? . . . I'm supposed to be on leave for the next three days . . . I understand, I can be at the airport in an hour."

Allen Cranfield, a 38-year-old former Salt Lake City police detective, lived with his wife and son. Allen grew up in Salt Lake City. He was a typical Mormon boy from a very affluent household. His father was a Professor of Biotechnology at the University of Utah, and his mother taught Psychology there. He played football in high school, served a two year mission for his churchwhen he was eighteen years oldin Germany. After his mission he married his high school sweetheart who had waited faithfully for him. He attended the University of Utah and received a degree in Criminal Justice, and a minor in Political Science. His parents were a bit disappointed as they always thought that he would go into either medicine or academia. At the age of twenty-six, he went to work for the Salt Lake City Police Department. Allen was a very handsome man. He stood at six feet three inches tall, was very fit and had thick dark hair that he wore short, and he had piercing blue eyes. Not only did he look like a policeman, he filled the role of a police officer very well. Allen was not satisfied with that, however. He wanted to be involved on a Federal level. So when the opportunity to apply for a position with Homeland Security came up, he jumped at the opportunity. With his schooling, his fluency in German, as well as his experience with the Police Department, he felt he was a shoe-in. He was not surprised when he got the call that he was hired, but he was a bit surprised when he was placed: The

Bioterrorism Counter-Intelligence Department. He was surprised also to find out that homeland security didn't mean what he thought it meant. He thought that homeland security meant to protect the United States against terrorism, but found that it was now a division of the World Government, under the direction of the United Nations, and its mission was to find threats, within the United States, against this World Government. Allen was very duty driven, though, and if this was the state of things, he was willing to serve. He loved what he did, and although he was working for a World Government, he still felt he was serving his country that he loved. His sense of duty to his profession made it difficult for him to be home with his wife and son as much as he would like. He loved his family, and felt that by being such a loyal officer, he was serving and taking care of his family. His job really became his identity, and he didn't have much time nor feel the need to devote much time to his religion, either. He had now been with Homeland Security's department of Bioterrorism Counter-Intelligence for five years.

Allen hung up the phone. He turned around to check on his wife, Holly, but was not surprised when he noticed that she was not in bed. Allen carefully walked around the end of his bed in the dark, reaching out for the wall to turn on the light. After turning on the light he went into the second bedroom where he found Holly sitting by the side of their six year-old son, Jack's bed.

"How is he doing?" Allen asked.

"The alarm went off at 6 A.M., I wanted to let you sleep in for once. I have had to suction his throat out two times since then. Who was on the phone?"

"The office", said Allen. "I have to go to Salt Lake City."

There was a long silence, and although Allen could not see his wife's face, he knew that she was not happy.

"I thought that you had three days off?"

"So did I," Allen said. "I guess the director of Homeland Security has asked for me specifically."

"When do you leave?" she asked.

"Right away, I have to be at the airport by 9 A.M.."

Allen walked over and put his hand on his wife's shoulder.

"I'm sorry Holly, I know that you are over-burdened here, but I really don't have a choice." Allen was sincere, but at the same time he felt a tremendous sense of pride in the fact that he was needed by his country. He would hate to have to turn down any assignment, for any reason. He leaned down and kissed her on the top of her head.

In the dimly lit room, Holly Cranfield sat next to her son's bed and cried quietly while her husband packed for his business trip. Holly had waited for Allen to return from his mission. There was never any doubt in her mind that they would be married. While waiting, she attended Salt Lake Community College and received an Associates degree in Early Childhood development. Waiting for

Allen was not easy. Holly was very attractive, and had quite a few young men chasing her while she was going to school. She even had one young man tell her that he was sure that she was the girl for him. She was sad to have to break his heart, but she knew it had to be Allen. When they were drawn in the lottery, and were allowed to have a child, Holly was a bit uneasy. She didn't like how the government had so much control over their lives, and always knew where they were and who they were with. It seemed that with the passage of time, it got worse and worse. She didn't remember it being like this at all when she was little. But with each year, there came new laws that lead to more government control. Holly remembered something that her father, a seminary teacher for the Mormon Church, told her as he was dying. "Beware of the mark." She kept her contempt for the government and their control secret from her husband. She knew that he would not understand. Allen was very pro-government programs, and wouldn't stand for anybody talking bad about it. He exercised control also in his home. He was the authority, and wouldn't stand for anything that would embarrass him in the public eye, and especially with his colleagues at work. When their son was born, he was a healthy baby. After his third set of vaccinations, Holly noticed a change in him. She tried to explain it to Allen, but he couldn't see it. Or maybe he just wouldn't allow himself to see it. It was as if she were accusing him of hurting their son. Then at the age of three, he started having seizures. They started slow, and then progressively got worse. At one point he had up to seventy seizures in one day. His doctors put him on very high doses of neuro-suppressive medications. They finally sedated him so much that he had to be placed on a respiratory monitor. When he got that bad, Holly felt that Allen had withdrawn even more from her and Jack. There now was this growing resentment inside of Holly. She resented the government for their control. She resented Allen for working for the government, and for not being there to protect Jack, and now not being there to help take care of him. She also hated feeling that she had to compete with the government for Allen's attention. Holly sat quietly by her son's bed, and considered leaving Allen while he was gone. She had thought about this for quite some time now, but was afraid due to her son's condition and Allen's position with the government. She knew that she could take care of Jack on her own because she had been doing it for so long, but she was concerned about money. Recently, she was contacted by her father-in-law. Allen had not spoken to his father or his mother for about four years, and they had not been allowed to see Jack or Holly. Allen never told Holly why, but she was not allowed to speak to his parents nor was she allowed to let them see Jack. Jack's father contacted Holly, and told her that if she ever needed any help they were there for her no matter what the situation was with Allen. Now Holly was seriously thinking about asking them to help her leave their son. *How would they react?* she wondered if they would hold to what they had said, but then again, she had always known her in-laws to keep their word. They had promised Allen that they would support him while he was going to school, and even though he was not pursuing the educational path that they wanted, and he got married before finishing school, they followed through and supported him, and her as well. They were always very gracious and loving toward Holly. She missed them. Holly's own parents divorced when she was young, and her Dad all but disappeared. She would see him once in a while for big events like weddings and funerals, but that was it. Holly was close to her Mom, however. She spoke with her on the telephone frequently, but since moving to Washington DC she never saw her. Holly's mom got by on very little, and had even had to get help from Holly and Allen a couple of times. This was difficult, as governement jobs didn't pay great. Allen was very tight with their spending and kept control of their funds. He would allow Holly a certain amount of money each paycheck to run the household, the rest he put into a savings account. He didn't like dipping into that to help his mother-in-law, but did it after Holly persuaded him.

As Allen arrived at the airport he was met by his boss, Alice Henderson, to brief him on why he was going to Salt Lake City. Alice Henderson was a forty-six year-old spinster daughter of a retired Army General. She graduated top of her class from M.I.T. with a Master's degree in Biological Engineering and a minor in Health Sciences and Technology. She was quickly snatched up by Homeland Security to work in the Bioterrorism Counter-Intelligence division, and after seventeen years, she was now the head of that division. Alice was a tall, very attractive, red head that anybody would find surprising that she was not married just by looking at her. But after getting to know her, it was clear why she had not yet been able to tie the knot. Although Alice has had many suitors, none could keep up with her intellectually, nor could they compete with the memory of her father. She was not afraid to let men know that either, and didn't seem to give it a minute's concern when she sent one packing. Alice had learned well from her father, who had easily made every boy that had ever called on Alice look like a blithering idiot. General Henderson was adept at the Socratic Method that within ten minutes of meeting a boy, the poor fellow didn't know what he believed. At first, this infuriated Alice, but eventually she found it quite amusing. Finally she started learning from her Dad and eventually mastered that skill, even surpassing her father. To say that Alice Henderson is cold would be like calling the sun a bit warm.

Allen shook hands with Alice as they greeted each other.

"Good morning, Director," Allen said.

"Good morning Agent Cranfield."

"So, what am I investigating in Salt Lake?" asked Allen.

"Oh, didn't my office tell you? I will be going with you. I'll brief you on the plane."

Allen was a little put out that he couldn't be trusted to handle this on his own, and he was also a bit nervous to be working in the field with the Director. He had never worked with her directly before, but he had heard horror stories.

One agent was fired within two hours of being on a case with her. So he had heard.

"Sounds good." Allen tried to sound confident. Allen and the Director entered the Learjet and sat across from each other with a table between them. After getting settled, a stewardess asked the Director if there was anything that they needed.

"Yes." She paused just long enough to turn her gaze to Allen. "Complete and undisturbed privacy."

Without even a flinch, the stewardess excused herself and entered a room toward the back of the plane. The director pushed a button on the table and a black screen came down in front of the door that the stewardess had entered and another one in front of the door to the cockpit. Allen knew that they could not be seen nor heard through those screens, and he also knew that whatever was going on was very serious.

"So, do you know why I have assigned you to this case Agent Cranfield?" the director asked.

"Well, I assumed it was because of my connections in Salt Lake City."

"Tell me agent Cranfield", the director's voice sounded like a trap getting ready to spring, "In what parts of your training were you taught to assume?"

Allen could feel his face and his neck getting hot, and he knew that he was flushing. "We work with what we know, Agent, and what we don't know, we find out. So what do we know about you?"

The director was leaning back in her leather chair with her legs crossed and her arms folded, looking into Allen's eyes like she was peering into his soul.

"Am I under investigation?" Allen asked incredulously.

"Should you be?"

"Hell no!"

Allen sat up in his chair. She pushed another button and a transparent hologram of a computer screen came up out of the table. After a few clicks a picture popped up on the screen, and Allen's heart began to race, his mouth went dry and he felt sick. Just then the plane began to taxi.

"Are you okay, Agent?"

"You look a little pale." The Director had a bit of an accusatory look on her face.

CHAPTER 5

SARAH FINISHED NURSING
Eric, Jr. and placed him on her chest
to burp him. As she sat in the quiet of her room, she noticed something on the
floor sticking out a little from under the leg of a chair in the corner. It looked like
a business card. After placing Eric, Jr. in his bassinet, she walked over to pick it up.
It was a business card, blank on the side that was up. As she flipped it over, she
saw the words:

There is still time to save your baby.

801-555-5555.

What in the world is this? Sarah thought. She walked back over to the bed and
sat on the edge of it. She stared at the card for a brief moment then picked up the
telephone and called the number.

"We're sorry, the number you have dialed is no longer in service, if you feel
you have reached this recording in error, please check the number and try your
call again."

Sarah hung up the phone and dialed the number again, getting the same
result. She placed the card on the table next to her bed and lied back in her bed.
She started to think of her Mom again. She had never known her, and had never
even seen a picture of her. Her Dad would not even tell Sarah her name. Now
that Sarah had a child of her own, she almost felt sympathy for her Mom. She
can understand a mother trying to protect her child from everything. Perhaps her
Dad had been a bit too harsh. Maybe her Mom just needed more time to realize
that the vaccinations were there to protect her child. Sarah felt sadness come over
her, and she started to weep. She wished that she could share the birth of her son
with her parents.

"It's not fair!" she whispered through her tears.

"Knock, knock!"

Sarah heard a familiar voice coming from the door. She quickly wiped the tears away from her eyes, and said, "Come in." It was Eric's mom and dad, Richard and Mary Dunn. Sarah was not particularly close with Eric's parents, but she was glad to see family. Sarah had always felt that Eric's parents tried to butt into their lives a little too much. In fact, it seemed as though Sarah was always hell bent on doing exactly the opposite of whatever her mother and father-in-law suggested on any topic. She just didn't want them to feel any satisfaction that they had swayed her and Eric in any way.

"Where's our new little grandson?" Eric's mom asked while rubbing her hands together like she was getting ready for a large feast.

Sarah took Eric, Jr. out of his basinet and placed him in Mrs. Dunn's waiting arms. As Richard and Mary swooned over their grandson, making all kinds of funny faces and noises, Sarah sat back and enjoyed the show. This was a side of Eric's parents that she had never seen. Usually they were so straight laced and polished Sarah was almost afraid to breath in front of them.

Richard looked up at Sarah and commented, "He is a handsome baby boy Sarah."

"Thank you." Just then, Richard's eyes caught a glimpse of the card that Sarah had sat on the table.

"What's this?" Richard asked as he reached over and picked it up. "There is still time to save your baby," he read out loud.

"What?!" Mary said with a shrill voice. "Sarah, what is this card?"

Sarah felt embarrassed and a bit indignant. She didn't know what it was, and she didn't like the accusatory look that her mother and father-in-law were giving her.

"I have no idea what that is. I found it on the floor just before you got here."

"Well, have you called this number?" Richard asked.

"It's disconnected," Sarah said while she nodded in the affirmative.

"I've heard of things like this on the news," Mary started in. "There are groups, secret groups that try to persuade people from having their babies vaccinated. Homeland Security calls them bio-terrorists and they have arrested a lot of them. The parents that get involved with them wind up going to prison and losing their children. It's really horrible."

Sarah paused for a moment before responding. "Why do you think they want to stop people from getting their babies vaccinated?"

"Crazies!" Mary said. "How can anyone know what they are thinking, or why."

Sarah thought of Mrs. Rasmussen, how she said that her baby was perfect, and then when they gave her shots, she saw the life drain from her. Sarah was grateful that Eric, Jr. did fine with his vaccinations. He didn't even seem to have any soreness in his legs where the shots were given, nor did he run a fever.

"Excuse me Mrs. Dunn." A nurse entering the room said. "We need to get you ready to take your baby upstairs to have his biostrip implanted."

Sarah didn't know why, but when she heard the nurse say that she got a sudden tickle in her stomach, and her heart began to race.

"Will it hurt him at all?"

The nurse was laying out some papers on the table, "There may be a little pain from the injection that they give him to numb the area, and when that medicine wears off there might be some mild discomfort. Don't worry, he will not remember it as he grows up."

Sarah looked over at her son who was lying in her mother-in-law's arms. "Can I hold him while they implant it?" Sarah asked.

"I'm sorry Mrs. Dunn, but the procedure and the device are highly classified. Only the Homeland Security medical team is allowed in the procedure room. Not even hospital staff are allowed."

Sarah didn't like that answer. She didn't feel comfortable with government goons doing some secret procedure on her son without her being there.

"I need you to sign these waivers before they can do the procedure," the nurse said.

"I would like to wait for my husband so that we can go over them together if you don't mind."

The nurse didn't look too happy, but she tried to pleasantly acknowledge Mrs. Dunn's request, and left the papers with her.

"I don't know why you don't just sign the waivers and get this over with." Mary said. "There is no telling when Eric will be here, and if they get backed up you may have to stay over another night. They won't release you until he has the biostrip."

Sarah knew that she made the right decision as soon as Mary spoke up, even if only to be contrary to Mary's thoughts.

"I'm sure Eric will be here soon." Sarah said. "Would you mind staying here with Eric, Jr. for a few minutes, I want to go check on another mother that gave birth the same day that I did."

"Go ahead," said Richard. "This will be our first of many babysitting gigs."

Sarah walked down to the nurse's station and asked about Mrs. Rasmussen.

"I'm sorry Mrs. Dunn, I don't show any record of a Mrs. Rasmussen. You say that she gave birth the same day as you?" Sarah was confused.

"She lost her baby!" Sarah said excitedly. "She came into my room just last night, and another nurse and two orderlies had to restrain her and take her back to her room. I just want to visit her to comfort her."

"Mrs. Dunn, the nurse said looking at her computer screen, there was only one baby delivered yesterday, and that was yours. There is no record of a Rasmussen. You must have been dreaming."

"I was *not* dreaming!" Sarah shouted.

Another nurse and an orderly stood up and approached the counter.

"What seems to be the problem?" the orderly asked.

Sarah started to get scared, and calmed herself down. She took a deep breath and then smiled. "Come to think of it, she said, I did have some pretty bizarre dreams last night. I guess that was one of them." Sarah excused herself and walked back to her room. Her head was spinning. She knew that she had not dreamt about Mrs. Rasmussen.

"That was fast," Mary said as Sarah entered the room.

"Oh, she has already been discharged." Sarah lied, not wanting to get into a lengthy discussion with Mary and Richard. "I need to nurse Eric, Jr. now, and then I think that I will take a nap. Thank you both for coming."

"Okay," said Richard. "It's time for us to go dear," he said to Mary who had a stunned look on her face. Mary handed Eric, Jr. over to Sarah and gave him a kiss on the cheek.

"Don't worry about anything when you get home Sarah, I will do all of the cooking and cleaning for a few days so that you can rest." Mary leaned in and gave Sarah a hug.

"Thank you" Sarah smiled.

Alone with her son, Sarah sat wondering what had happened to Mrs. Rasmussen. *Why would they not have any record of her?* she thought. *I know that she was here.* Sarah laid Eric, Jr., who was asleep now, in his bassinet, and then lied down in her bed to take a nap.

CHAPTER 6

A S ERIC WALKED through the front door of the mansion, he felt dwarfed by the size of the front entry. The floor was a beautiful white marble that went on to create six foot wide hallways down both sides of a ten foot wide staircase that went up twelve steps to a landing that had stairs going up on each side to a larger landing which extended the entire width of the entryway and ended at wide hallways on either side. On each side of the entryway was a large twelve foot high maple doorway that entered into another room. The door to his right was closed, and the door to his left was open. James escorted him to the door on his left. As he entered the room he noticed the warmth of the décor. It had a pool table at one end of the large room, and at the other end, a large horseshoe shaped leather sofa with a large coffee table in the center. On the wall, directly in front of the sofa was a sixty inch flat screen TV that was bordered by book shelves containing movies and video games. This was obviously a family recreation room. In the middle of the room, between the pool table and the TV area, the wall jutted out to create a little nook that could be cordoned off from the rec room by closing two glass French doors. In this room was a small table and a couple of high backed burgundy leather easy chairs. The walls were covered with books that were neatly kept on bookshelves that extended to the ceiling. *The library*, Eric thought to himself. The coloring in these rooms was warm, as was the temperature, and soft lighting made Eric feel very comfortable, also.

Eric sat down in one of the easy chairs. He was amazed at the beauty of this mansion. He had never seen anything like it, except in movies, and with the world economy as it was he didn't think houses like this existed.

"Hello Mr. Dunn," a soft male voice said from the doorway behind Eric.

Eric quickly stood up and turned to see who was speaking. He saw an elderly gentleman who stood about six feet tall. He was clean shaven and well groomed, and was wearing tan slacks with a cannery yellow long sleeve shirt that was well starched, ironed, and looked great with his crystal clear blue eyes. He had a very pleasant look on his face, and Eric felt an instant connection with him.

"Hello", Eric replied. "Sebastian?"

"My name is Henry. Sebastian was the name of my lab rat. I'm glad that you were able to find my home."

"Well if I hadn't had the address, I'm sure that I would never have known this house existed. You are well hid back here."

"Yes," Henry said, "Well hid from some, but from others there is no hiding."

There was a moment of awkward silence as both men thought about the implications of what Henry had just said.

"Well, I'm sure that you have many questions, and this is a good time and a good place to get them answered. Please, sit down."

Eric sat back down in the chair that he had gotten up from, and Henry sat in the chair that was next to him. The chairs were slightly slanted so that the backs were far enough apart to allow a small table and lamp to stand there, and close enough in front and angled enough to be able to see each other and have a nice conversation.

"Mr. Dunn," Henry started, "Let me ask you a question. Why do you think that slavery was abolished?"

Eric thought that that was a very curious question to start with given the events of the last twenty-four hours.

"Well, because it was an evil and immoral act perpetrated by our ancestors", Eric replied.

"Yes Mr. Dunn, it was evil and immoral. But I believe that the reason was abolished is because the blacks knew that they were slaves. If they never had known that they were slaves then they would probably still be in bondage today. Do you think, Mr. Dunn, that it is possible to enslave a group of people without them knowing it?"

"No, I don't believe that it is."

"Well Mr. Dunn, I'm here to tell you that it is not only possible, it has been done to the entire human race. The American people cry freedom. They hold freedom up on a banner. But if you create a cause, if you give them a perceived threat, it doesn't even have to be a real threat. If they perceive a threat, they will toss liberty in a heartbeat for security from that perceived threat. You see, all you need to do is to have an apparent threat to people, then you can offer a solution. This will create a cause that, if the majority of the population get behind it, will allow you to put all of the people in bondage, and they will not even know it. For instance, years ago before you were born, most people in the United States owned guns. In fact, many owned military style guns. There were some very sick and bad people who killed many innocent people with these weapons. This created a threat, and the government offered a solution, which was to outlaw these types of weapons. The majority of the people agreed, and so we lost the right to own these types of weapons. Later, it became easy to use the same strategy to take away all privately owned weapons."

"Well how is that bondage?" Eric asked.

"That was just the beginning. Using the threat of epidemic illnesses, the government was able to bring about mandatory vaccinations. Using the threat of identity theft, the government was able to bring about the use of the bioscanner. Using the threat of worldwide economic disaster, the government was able to bring about the international currency credit that has the same value worldwide."

"These all seem like good things to me", said Eric.

"That is exactly what they want you to think Mr. Dunn."

"Do you mean the government?" Eric asked.

"No, I mean those who control the governments. It is they who have used the well meaning government officials to take liberties from us and put us into their servitude. It is they that profit from us, just as the plantation owners profitted from the slaves. The only difference is that we don't know that we are slaves. Each vaccine that is sold makes them a profit. Each medication that is taken to treat the side affects of the vaccination makes them a profit. Each insurance premium makes them a profit. Each time you scan your bioscanner to transfer a UCC they make a profit. All of this was by their design, and it is slavery. The bioscanner is our shackle."

Eric sat quietly, trying to take this all in. His story all fit together nicely, but Eric found it hard to believe that people all over the world would be so naive. To think that he and his family, and everyone that he knows had been in bondage his whole life? It didn't seem plausible.

"How do you know all of this?"

"Because, Mr. Dunn, I invented the bioscanner, and by it, I caught a glimpse into their little circle."

Eric wondered about the biostrip, and how he called it a shackle.

"Henry, tell me about the biostrip. How is that our shackle?"

Henry leaned back and put both hands on top of his head like he was being arrested. He looked up at the ceiling and took in a deep breath.

"I was doing research, trying to design a diagnostic tool that would allow doctors to, well, kind of see inside your body without doing an expensive MRI, or a CT scan. The problem that I was having is that the device that I had designed to be implanted inthe body was too big. It had to be in order to monitor all of the systems, and be able to transmit the information without having to be plugged in. I had a colleague, Dr. Akim Berkovits. He was, or rather is, an entomologist. I was just talking with him about the difficulty that I was having, and he made an off the cuff, facetious statement that changed everything. He said, 'It's too bad that you can't somehow link it with the nervous system, thereby making it nothing more than a transmitter of what the nervous system already monitors.' I was intrigued by this, and asked him to expound. He said, 'Look at the insect world. They can tell if another bug is sick or wounded just by picking up what the bug is transmitting.' I then began researching the possibility of bioengineering a living organism that had the transmitting and receiving capacity of an insect's nervous system and implanting it into the body and having it connect with the nervous system. This proved to be fairly easy, but my biggest problem was that the body saw the foreign matter as a virus, and destroyed it. After about three years of work, I finally came up with an organism that had nervous tissue from a cockroach combined with the alimentary organs of a leech and masked by human tissues that, with the use of proper immunosupressant medication, would not be rejected. This organism is about the size of a cricket, it has no legs, so it moves much like a worm or caterpillar. It acts more like a synergist with the body than it does a parasite. It has very slow metabolism, so its demand on the host blood is very low. Its tail sucker is adapted to send axons into the host nervous system and in essence, link itself to the host. Sebastian was my first test subject with the new specimen. He did not reject it. I was able to create a receiver using the same material that could be connected to a sophisticated computer. We were able to monitor all of his major body systems. Because a rat's actions are similar to a cockroach's, in that they avoid open, well lit places, we did not recognize another side effect until we implanted a chimpanzee. We found out that the implant pretty much dominated the nervous system. The chimp was photophobic, and seemed a bit paranoid. We found that we could reduce this effect by lowering the body temperature of the host. What is the normal body temperature of a human Mr. Dunn?"

Eric was startled by the question,. He had been so engrossed in the story.

"92.3 degrees Fahrenheit" Eric replied.

"Actually Mr. Dunn, the physiologically normal body temperature is 98.6 degrees. That 6.3 degree difference is what is needed to prevent the insect nervous tissue from dominating your nervous system. That is why you have felt a bit sick, and photophobic yourself lately. Your failure to take your meds has allowed your body temperature to rise."

"Wait a minute!" Eric held up his hands as if to hold back what Henry was telling him. "Are you saying that there is insect . . . . Cockroach tissue in my body?"

"I'm afraid so." Henry said apologetically. "The biostrip implanted in every human being is a micro chip that contains your personal information, UCC account balance, travel history, vehicle information, address, and employment information. It also keeps track of everytime your scanner is picked up in a public place where there are scanners. Along with the microchip implanted in your wrist, there is insect nervous tissue implanted in the back of your neck, just below the base of the skull."

Eric reached back and rubbed the back of his neck feeling for a scar. There was a very small one that he had never noticed or paid any attention to. It would not be visible because it was just above the hairline. Eric's skin began to crawl as he realized what was inside of him.

"We also discovered", Henry continued, "That people whose temperatures raise to normal can not only transmit information, but can also receive information from others. The government uses this knowledge in its Homeland Security leaders to be able to detect lies. You may have noticed, now that you have not been taking your meds, that you are able to detect things from others."

"Yes!" Eric said excitedly. "But I have not detected anything from you or James."

Henry smiled, "No, and you won't, because we have had our biostrips removed. Just as you will have yours removed."

Eric sat there in awe, not knowing what to say. Gradually that shock turned to rage, then to worry for his son.

Eric stood up, "I've got to get to the hospital!"

"Don't worry", Henry said, "I have people there. They won't implant your son without us knowing long before it happens."

Just then James walked into the room holding the telephone in his hands. "I'm sorry to interupt sir, but you have a call that I know you will want to take."

Henry stood and took the telephone, "Excuse me", he said to Eric. He stepped into the rec room just out of ear shot.

"Hello, this is Henry."

"Henry it's me. You need to know that a Homeland Security team left for Salt Lake this morning."

Henry hesitated for a moment then asked, "Is he with them?"

"Yes he is."

Henry got a lump in his throat, "Well I guess they will be coming here then. What time did they leave?"

"Sometime around 7 this morning. Your time."

Henry turned with a start toward James and motioned him to get rid of Eric's car.

"They will be here anytime then." Henry said, "What are your plans?"

He listened intently, then replied, "I understand. I will have people there within the hour, get ready." Henry hung up the telephone, and then placed another call. He waited for an answer.

"Hello, this is Henry. I need you to make the move that we talked about. Yes, within the hour. Thank you." Again he hung up the phone and then placed another call. "Its time." Was all that he said, and then he hung up the telephone and went back to the library where Eric was waiting.

Eric sat in silence by himself pondering on everything that had been going on. *How did all of this happen, and how have I been so naive my entire life?* he wondered. Eric resolved at that point that he would not allow this to happen to his son. For the first time in his life, Eric cared. Then he started to wonder how it is possible to get along in this world where the biostrip is used for everything, if you do not have a biostrip. Just then Henry returned.

"Mr. Dunn, there has been a developement. We need to take you to a secure location right away."

"What about my wife and son?" "I have already made a call, they will meet you later."

Henry led Eric through the game room, then through the entry way to a hallway on the other side. Henry closed the door to the hallway after they entered it.

"Mr. Dunn, I knew that this day would eventually come. Homeland Security has discovered my operation, and are on there way here now. I don't want you to panic, though, because I have prepared for this. Please stand in the center of the hallway and brace yourself."

Henry reached up to a picture on the wall, and turned it counter clockwise. Suddenly the small section of the hallway that they stood in began to lower and Eric soon found himself facing a cement wall. They continued to lower for what seemd like quite a while, and finally Eric found himself facing a metal elevator door. The door opened and they exited the elevator. James was standing just outside the elevator, and handed each of them a heavy jacket. Eric was glad, because it was quite cold where they were.

"Is everything prepared?" Henry asked James.

"Yes sir, we are all clear."

Henry opened a cover on a key pad on the wall to his left, and entered a twelve digit code.

He hesitated for a second, and asked James, "Are you sure?"

James nodded and Henry hit enter. They both turned quickly and started down the long, dimly lit cement hallway. Eric followed.

"What is going on?" Eric asked.

"We are evacuating," Henry replied. "I have just detonated a large explosion and fire that will destroy my entire home and any evidence that might be in there."

They continued to walk down this hallway for what seemed like twenty minutes. Finally they came to another elevator. Henry entered another code on a key pad by the door, and it opened. They entered the elevator, and after the door closed they automatically began to go up. Again, it seemed like quite a long ascent. When the elevator doors opened, they were in a large abandoned building, and Eric could see a busy street through some large windows at the front of the building. Henry turned and opened another key pad on the wall by the elevator doors. He entered another code, and only paused briefly before pushing enter. Henry and James again began walking quickly to the front of the building, Eric followed in silence. They exited the building, and entered a red Toyota Camry that was waiting by the curb just outside. The driver didn't say anything, he just waited for them all to get in and then drove off.

CHAPTER 7

S ARAH HAD JUST started to doze when a nurse entered her room and woke her.

"I'm sorry Mrs. Dunn, but we are going to be moving you and your son to another room on another floor. We will not be able to implant your baby's biostrip until tomorrow, so you will be staying over night."

Sarah asked, "Can I call my husband to let him know?"

"I'm not quite sure what room we will be puting you in until we get to the nurses station on that floor, so why don't you wait until we get you there to give him a call?"

Sarah nodded and agreed. The nurse helped Sarah into a wheelchair, and then pushed the bassinet in front of Sarah so she could push it while the nurse pushed Sarah. They entered an elevator, and the nurse closed the door. Sarah watched as the nurse pushed the "B3" button.

"What floor is "B3" Sarah asked.

Just then Sarah felt a sharp pain in the side of her neck, and almost immediately felt dizzy, and although she tried to resist, she fell asleep.

Sarah woke up in a hospital bed, confused and disoriented at first. She looked around to try to recall her location, and then remembered that the last thing that happened was entering an elevator with a nurse, then feeling a sharp pain in her neck and then feeling very dizzy. Sarah sat up quickly.

"Eric!" she exclaimed. Then she saw the bassinet next to her bed, and inside she saw her baby boy. She reached down to pick him up, and the whole room shoock.

"Earthquake!"

Sarah gasped, she picked up Eric, Jr. and walked quickly toward the door. The door would not open no matter how hard she tried. She quickly went back to her bed and pushed the nurses call button.

A male voice came over the speaker, "May I help you?"

"I think that we are having an earthquake, and I can't open my door." Sarah answered, and then wondered why he seemed so calm in the middle of an earthquake. There was a little bit of a pause, then the male voice came on again, "The nurse will be right with you."

Sarah was shocked. They were obviously having an earthquake and nobody seemed to care. She went to the window to look to see if others were evacuating, and when she pulled the curtain open she saw that there was no window. Just a wall with a light behind an opaque white, square piece of plastic made to look like a window behind the curtain. Sarah began to panic, then realized that the earthquake seemed to be going on for a long time. The more that she thought about how it felt, the more she realized that what she was feeling was the movement of a vehicle on a road. She was not in a building, but in a vehicle. Just then, the door opened. The nurse that came to move her to a different room walked in with a smile on her face.

"Mrs. Dunn, are you okay?" the nurse asked. Sarah looked at her in fear, wondering who she was and why she had taken her.

"Who are you, and where are you taking me?" Sarah demanded.

"My name is Joan, and we are taking you somewhere safe." she replied.

"Safe! Safe from what?" Sarah asked. Just then a red light on the wall by the door turned on, and Joan said, "Everything will be explained to you shortly, just know that you and your baby are in no danger, and you will be joining your husband shortly." With that, Joan walked out of the door. *Eric!* Sarah thought, *I can call Eric.* Sarah put Eric, Jr. down, and quickly looked through her purse for her cell phone. She pushed the speed dial button for Eric's phone, but nothing happened. She tried it again, and still nothing happened."

Mary, I'll call Mary."

Again, when she pushed the speed dial button for her mother-in-law, nothing happened. She then looked at the top of the screen on her smart phone and realized that she didn't have any service. She quickly went to the phone by her bed. She picked it up and dialed Eric's cell number. After one ring she heard the phone pick up.

"Eric help me!" she started but then realized that she was hearing a recording on the other end.

"The number you have dialed is no longer in service."

She hung up and redialed, thinking that she had misdialed. Again she got a recording. She tried her mother-in-law's phone, and got the same recording. In despair, she slammed the phone down. She was scared, and now Eric, Jr. was crying. She picked him up and sat down to nurse him. He stopped crying immediately. While she sat there nursing him, she tried to figure out what might be going on. *Joan said that I would be joining Eric soon.* she thought to herself. *Joining him where, though?* Sarah wondered if this could have anything to do with the strange card that she had found on the floor in her room. She finished nursing Eric, Jr., burped him, then she changed his diaper and put him back down in the bassinet.

I have got to find a way out of here, she thought as she began looking around the room.

The bedside telephone rang. She looked at it like it was a large spider. After the third ring, she picked up the receiver. She didn't say hello, but just listened. After a moment of silence, she heard "Sarah?" It was Eric's voice.

"Eric!" she said excitedly. "Where are you? They have taken me and Eric, Jr. somewhere. I don't know where we are," Sarah began to cry.

"Sarah, it is okay. I asked them to come get you, because you were not safe at the hospital. They are bringing you to me."

"I don't understand," Sarah said in confusion. "Why was I not safe at the hospital?"

"Sarah, I have learned some pretty amazing things in the last eighteen hours and I made a decision to not allow the government to enslave our son, and I am getting you and I out of bondage, also."

"Eric, you are not making any sense to me."

Eric told Sarah that he would see her in a couple of hours and would explain everything to her, then the phone went dead. Sarah hung up the phone, and sat there with her head spinning. She was not so frightened anymore, but she began to grow angry with Eric. How could he do this without talking to her first? Sarah thought of her Dad, and began to understand what he did. She used to think that maybe he had been a bit harsh, but now she was thinking that he had done the right thing. Sarah began to plan how she would save her son and herself from her husband's madness. She decided that the first chance she got, she would get away and call the police.

Sarah felt the vehicle that she was in come to a stop. She wondered if they had arrived at their location yet, and if she would be seeing Eric soon. After about ten minutes, she felt them begin to move again. Another couple of minutes passed and the door to her room opened. Another nurse came in. She was older than the nurse that had kidnapped her and Eric, Jr. Sarah recognized her, but she wasn't quite sure where she had seen her before. Then it dawned on her, she was there in the delivery room.

"Hello Sarah," the nurse said with a kindly voice and a sweet smile. Sarah was shocked at how the nurse's voice made her feel. It was as though she had known this nurse her entire life.

"My name is Clare. I was there when Eric, Jr. was born. Do you remember me?" Sarah nodded.

"May I hold him?" Clare asked. Sarah looked at her in silence for a moment then softly said, "No."

Nodding her head, Clare said, "I understand. You are no doubt frightened, and unsure of what is going on or where you are."

"So, where am I?" Sarah asked. Clare was looking at Eric, Jr with a longing look in her eyes. She looked up at Sarah, sighed and said, "You are in a large mobile home on Interstate 80, just outside of Laramy, Wyoming."

Sarah was startled by her frank answer.

"Why?" Sarah asked quietly.

Clare looked at Sarah in silence for a long moment then said, "I'm not sure how much information you can, or will be willing to, accept right now, so let me say that your husband made a decision to not have Eric, Jr. vaccinated or implanted, and has asked us to help you all be safe from the government. I will let Eric tell you more when we pick him up."

Sarah was grateful for the candid information.

"When will we be picking up Eric?"

"We are scheduled to meet up with them in about an hour."

"Them?" Sarah asked.

"Eric is with a dear friend of mine, Henry, who has made all of this possible."

"Have you done this before?"

Clare sat down in the rocking chair.

"We have helped hundreds of people get out of bondage, but we have never had to evacuate anyone before."

Sarah got a little scared, then asked "Why are we being evacuated?"

Clare stared into Sarah's eyes intently for a moment then said, "Because we have been discovered by Homeland Security, we are all evacuating."

Sarah's rage began to build.

"You are going to cause me to lose my son!"

Clare held her hands up and said, "We have prepared for this. You will not get caught. Even if you did, you could claim that this was all done against your will."

"Which it was!" Sarah said.

"Right," Clare replied.

There was a moment of silence.

Clare asked Sarah, "Would you tell me about your family?"

"What family are you talking about?" Sarah asked.

"Your Dad, and Mom, and any siblings."

"I didn't have any siblings, my parents divorced when I was a baby and I was raised by my Dad."

"You didn't ever see your Mom?"

"No. She was a criminal, like all of you, and she was put in prison."

"What did she do?"

"She tried to do what you are all trying to do right now. She tried to not have me vaccinated."

Clare stared at Sarah in silence, "Why do you think she did that Sarah?"

"Because she was crazy, and thought that the government was out to get us just like you do." Sarah was very curt and cold in her answers as though she was trying to really hurt Clare.

"I know that you don't believe what we say about the government, but isn't it possible that your mother did what she did out of love for you?" There was a break in Clare's voice, and Sarah could see a glisten in her eyes. She felt some vindication because she was trying to cause her pain, but then she realized that she was not choked up because of Sarah's hurtful remarks, but she was choking up because of Sarah's mother's actions.

"Why do you care what happened to my mother?" Sarah asked.

"What did happen to your mother?" asked Clare.

"I told you, she went to prison."

"That was over twenty-five years ago. Surely she is out by now. Have you not ever heard from her?"

"No, and I've always wondered why. I have thought about looking her up, but when she was arrested they removed her information from my birth records, and my Dad would never talk about it. I don't even know her name."

"What would you like to say to her?" asked Clare.

"I don't know. I guess that I would just like to know what she is like. I have always had this picture in my head of this ratted haired, ill-kept crazy woman in tattered clothes and two front teeth missing. I would like to know where she got the crazy idea to try to prevent me from being vaccinated."

Clare sat in silence for a while just looking down at her hands asSarah tended to Eric, Jr.

Finally Clare looked up, "Sarah, if someone you loved was in bondage, a slave, would you try to free them?"

"Yes, if I could." Sarah replied.

"What if they didn't believe that they were in bondage?"

Sarah thought for a while, then said, "Well, if they didn't know that they were in bondage, and they were happy, then I don't know if I would. I mean, if someone doesn't know what they are missing, then they really aren't missing it are they?"

"So, even if you knew that they were living in bondage, and that freedom would allow them to experience so much more of life, you would leave them in bondage?" asked Clare.

Sarah answered, "I heard of a lady that was deaf from childhood. She was a wife, and a mother of five, yet she never knew what her husband or children sounded like. She was given the opportunity to receive a cochlear implant that would allow her to hear. She was so excited. She had the operation, and was told that it would take some time to get used to it. She would need to learn what the sounds meant. After two years of misery trying to know what each sound she heard was, she removed the outside part of her implant and never put it on again. She was happier not hearing. So don't you think that if a person is happy with their situation, you are better off not letting them know what they do not have?"

Clare pulled a newspaper clipping out of her pocket and handed it to Sarah. Sarah unfolded the clipping and read it.

"Young couple and their unborn child were killed in a car crash on their way to the hospital." Under the headline was a picture of a mangled car. "Do you think that Sharlene Rasmussen was better off not knowing the truth?" Clare asked.

"Who is Sharlene Rasmussen?" asked Sarah.

"Mrs. Rasmussen was in the hospital giving birth the same day that you were. Her baby did not survive the vaccinations."

Sarah's heart came up into her throat and she felt the hair on the back of her head stand up, as she remembered the sad figure standing in her room that night with anguish in her eyes. She also remembered how the nurses told her that there was no "Mrs. Rasmussen".

Sarah looked up at Clare, "I understand." She said.

CHAPTER 8

"WE HAVE REASON to believe that this man, your father, is the head of a bioterrorist organization known as the C.T.D.O. Their main objective is to help people work outside the system and be able, if they so choose, to not have their vaccinations and not get their children vaccinated." said the Director to Allen Cranfield, who was still in shock by the picture that he was looking at. Allen did not respond, but just stared at the picture.

"Agent Cranfield!" said Director Harrison rather forcefully.

This startled Allen back to the moment, and he looked at the Director.

"Ma'am?"

"Agent, I brought you on this assignment for two reasons, one because he is your father and I need to know if you are involved, and two, because he is your father and you may be a valuable asset. So, I need to know agent Cranfield, and I will know if you lie, whose side are you on?"

Allen's answer was quick and to the point. "I am on the side of our country, Ma'am. I have not been on the best of terms with my father for quite some time. I think that I can help in this matter. May I make a quick phone call?"

The director peered into Allen's eyes for a moment, and then asked, "Who do you need to call, and why?"

"Ma'am due to the position that I hold, and my father being who he is and because of our strained relationship, I have had a wire tap put on my home phone for quite some time. I need to find out if there have been any calls between him and my wife."

"Do you suspect that your wife is involved somehow?"

"No, but my relationship with my wife has been a bit strained, and I know that my Dad has offered to help her leave me. If he thinks that we are coming for him, he will try to run and take her and my son."

The Director replied, "That may be difficult given your son's condition. Anyway, we have been watching your family also, and in fact there was a call placed early this morning from your phone to your father's."

"Ma'am, I think that we need to get a unit over to my house right away to monitor the situation."

"Well ahead of you agent," said the Director, "And I'm glad that you are playing on the right team. So, what can you tell me about Dr. Henry Cranfield?"

"I can tell you that my Dad is very intelligent and lives life like a game of chess. He is always planning several steps ahead in every aspect of his life. After he invented the biostrip, things got crazy. He seemed very paranoid and actually accused me of being part of the enforcement organization for an elite world super power. This is what caused our falling out. I told him that he was crazy, and that I didn't want him scaring my wife. I asked him to stop coming around."

There was a red light blinking on the telephone next to the computer.

The Director picked it up, "I didn't want to be disturbed" she said with a short tone. "Well then, what is it? I see, what time? Thank you." She hung up the phone. "Does your dad have any guns or explosives?" Allen looked worried, "No, not that I know of. Why?"

"There has been a large explosion completely leveling your father's home. As far as we know, your father was in the house with another man. We might be going back to a funeral agent Cranfield."

"It could be part of an attempt to cover his tracks, Ma'am. I told you that he started to get real spooky after the biostrip."

"Where do you think he would be going?"

"Well, as I said, I have been out of contact for quite a while. There was an old cabin just outside of a little town in Colorado that my grandfather built. I think that it is called Glen Echo. It is located on state Hwy 14, west of Fort Collins up the Poudre Canyon."

The Director picked up the telephone, "Get me the Fort Collins office." There was a pause, then she said, "This is Director Henderson . . . security clearance code alpha one November six three niner beta delta six." She paused again while taking out a security code key fob from her coat pocket. "Authentication sugar beat" . . . I need a team up the Poudre Canyon to a town called Glen Echo. Get a camp site and pose as tourists. I will send a secure fax with the target data. I also need you to contact the Salt Lake office, forward the target information to them and have them alert the TSA at the Salt Lake Airport. This is a level five threat. Report directly to me or Agent Allen Cranfield if there is any activity. Do not attempt any contact with the target. Do you understand?"

After a short pause she hung up the telephone. She looked up at Allen and said, "I think that we should continue on to Salt Lake, and see what information we can gather there." Just then another light began to flash on the telephone. The Director picked it up, "Yes?I see . . . How far from the first explosion? I want traffic cams from that area scanned. If a mouse came out of that building, I want to know what color it was."

"What happened? asked Allen.

"A building fire broke out one and a half miles away from your Dad's house just thirty-five minutes after the explosion at your dad's home. It looks like you were right, Agent. Your Dad is trying to cover his tracks."

"You said that my dad was in the house with another man right?"

"Yes, why?"

"My dad has a personal assistant named James. Do we know if that was the man?"

"No, all I know is that there was another man in the house. We have a satellite image of the two of them entering the house."

"Wait a minute, you say that the image showed two of them entering the house, was it from the driveway?"

"Yes."

"That could not have been my Dad. Ever since he got all paranoid, he would only enter the house through the garage. He didn't want any of us seeing him."

"Then, who were the two men entering your dad's house?"

"I don't know who one of them was, but the other would have been James. He would escort all visitors into the house. My Dad also had a security detail. He had three armed men with large dogs. They stayed in a separate building away from the home. Do we know anything about them?"

"No. I will have our lead team find out more and they can fill us in when we arrive." The Director picked up the phone and said, "Get me the Salt Lake Office." After a pause she said, "This is Director Henderson, security clearance code alpha one November six three niner beta delta six." She then reached for her fob again, pushed the button on it and said, "Authentication speed boat." She waited just a second and said, "I want to be put in touch with the team investigating the Cranfield explosion." Another pause and she said, "This is Director Harrison. Agent Cranfield and I are en route. We should be wheels down in approximately two hours. Agent Cranfield tells me that there was a guard detail on the premises; they had quarters away from the main house. Check that out, and be careful. They are armed. Also see if we can get a license plate on the car that we picked up by satellite." She hung up the phone. Just as she did, the light began to flash again. She picked it up, "Yes." She listened for a moment, "Ok, stay on them and keep me informed."

She hung up the phone, "A medical transport just showed up at your house, and they are loading your son and wife in right now."

"Damn!" Allen said.

"Does your wife know about the bug that you had on the phone?"

"No," Allen answered.

"What about the government personnel monitoring system in your apartment? Does she know about that?"

"Of course not." Allen said.

The light on the telephone began flashing again.

"This is Director Henderson." She listened for a moment then said, "I have Agent Cranfield with me right now. Let me put you on speaker phone."

She pushed a button on the phone and said, "Go ahead."

"Yes Ma'am," Allen heard a male voice say over the speaker. "We have followed the medical transport to a parking garage at a mall in D.C. We have men at each exit of the garage. Do you want us to move in?"

"Well, I doubt that they are going shopping!" Allen said with a raised voice.

"Yes sir," The man replied over the speaker.

"You better get a team in there," the director said. "Be careful, you are dealing with a young boy on life support. If you don't feel that you can make an apprehension without the use of deadly force, than stay back and wait for the right time."

"Yes Ma'am . . . Will do."

The Director hung up the phone. As soon as she did, the light began flashing again. This time she didn't bother picking it up, but went straight to the speaker button.

"This is Director Henderson and Agent Cranfield, go ahead."

"Yes ma'am, this is Agent Bowen in Salt Lake. We have the information that you requested on the vehicle at Dr. Cranfield's home."

"Well go ahead agent Bowen, let's have it," the director said.

Allen took out a pen and pad to take some notes.

"It is registered to an Eric and Laura Dunn." Agent Bowen said.

"What else?" asked the Director.

"Just their address Ma'am . . . There is no criminal background at all."

"Ok, get a search warrant and get over there. We will be on the ground in a couple of hours. I want some answers."

"Yes Ma-," the director cut agent Bowen's answer off by hanging up the phone. "Does the name Eric Dunn ring a bell?" the director asked Allen.

"I was just thinking about that," he responded. "It does not ring a bell at all, but like I said, I have been out of my father's loop for quite some time and I'm sure that with all of the radical stuff he has been into, he has made alliances with many different people that I would not know."

CHAPTER 9

HOLLY CRANFIELD HUNG up the phone after speaking with her father-in-law. She didn't say much, just, "He's on his way, and I'm ready." He acknowledged that and said good bye. Holly went to work packing and preparing her son. Five minutes later, the telephone rang.

"Hello?"

A man on the other end of the phone spoke, "Mrs. Cranfield, this is your transport. Henry asked me to contact you and tell you that we will be there within the hour. Please be ready, Ma'am. We do not have time to waste."

"I understand", she said, "I will be ready."

She hung up the phone and continued her preparations. She packed food for her son, and clothing for the both of them. Then she went into her husband's computer desk and copied all of the files onto a thumb drive. She filled a small bucket from under the kitchen sink with Sulfuric acid. She then removed the hard drive from the computer and dropped it into the bucket. She removed a couple of paper files from the computer desk drawer and ran them through a shredder. She then took the shredded paper to the stove and in a small frying pan she burned it. She then removed a large box from the top shelf of her pantry that concealed a digital video recorder. She unplugged it from its leads and took out a barrel key to remove its hard drive. She dropped that into the bucket of acid also. She removed her cell phone from her purse and removed its SIM card and battery. She dropped the SIM card into the bucket of acid, as well. She took out a balloon and filled it with gasoline, and tied it to a piece of string hanging over the bucket of acid. She then moved her son into a transport chair. Just then her door bell rang.

She pushed the intercom, "Who is it?".

A man replied, "We are here, Ma'am."

She pushed the button unlocking the outside door to let them into the building. Within thirty seconds they were at her door. Two men came in and went right to work taking her things out. They made one trip with her bags, then returned for her son. After taking her son down, one of the men came back for her.

"Do you have everything ready?" he asked.

"Yes, I do." she said.

Then he turned and walked out. Holly followed, but paused at the front door just long enough to toss her cell phone battery into the bucket of acid. She shut the door and went to the elevator. The acid ate away at the battery until the lithium came in contact with the acid causing a small explosion, which ignited the balloon of gasoline. The balloon exploded into a fire ball and spread flames all over the room. By the time Holly reached the transport van, the fire alarm was sounding in her apartment. They drove without speaking to *The Shops at 2000 Penn Shopping Mall* and entered the parking garage. They found a parking spot on the bottom level in a darkened corner.

As soon as they stopped, the driver took a walkie talkie out of his shirt pocket, pushed the speak button and said, "Bottom level, Orange 27."

A voice came over the radio, "Copy.".

He put the radio back into his pocket and they got out of the car. The men went to work on the outside of the car removing magnetic signs that read *Holy Cross Medical Transport.* They then removed a thin cellophane covering that covered the entire van making it look light blue. After that they changed the license plates. By this time, another unmarked, black van pulled up. They moved all of Holly's things into the black van. Then they moved Jack into the black van, too. Holly sat in the back by Jack to tend to his needs. One of the two men that picked her up stayed at the mall, while the other went with her and the driver of the black van. They did all of this like a well choreographed dance, with very littleconversation.

Once they had left the garage, the man in the front passenger seat turned to her and said, "Ma'am, my name is Kirk . . . This is Bill. We will be taking you to meet Henry. We have a long trip. Please feel free to let us know if there is anything that you need. We will make stops only for gas, unless you say something."

Holly smiled and said, "Thank you. Can you tell me where we will be meeting Henry?"

"No Ma'am, I don't know yet. Our instructions were to get onto Interstate 66 and head west. We will receive instructions before we hit Interstate 81."

After about thirty minutes of riding in silence, Kirk's cell phone rang.

"Hello. Yes sir." Kirk pushed a button on his phone and put it on speaker mode. Then Kirk said, "Go ahead sir."

Holly heard Henry's voice next.

"Holly, can you hear me?"

"Yes, Henry."

"Good. I trust that you and Jack are okay. You are in good hands with Kirk and Bill. Now Kirk, I want you to follow the 'Jack Gregory' route."

"I understand", Kirk replied.

"I will speak with you all soon. Goodbye."

The phone went dead. Holly looked at Kirk with a questioning look, "Jack Gregory route?" she said.

"He wants us to take Highway 70", Kirk replied. "Why Jack Gregory? asked Holly.

"Jack Gregory played for the Cleveland Browns, and is considered the 70th all time greatest player to ever play for them."

"Oh, I see."

Kirk turned on the radio so they could listen to the news.

"The five alarm Andover apartment fire on N street is still blazing. Officials still are unsure what the cause of the fire was. I have Fire Chief McClusky here . . . Chief, have there been any injuries?"

"No. Thank God. The fire alarm got everybody up and out."

"I hear rumors, Chief, that this fire is burning way too hot and fast for a building of this type. Can you comment on that?"

"Well, I can't say for certain, and so I better not comment at this time. We will know more when we get this out."

The station news caster came back on, "In related news, police have issued an Amber alert for Jack Cranfield, a six year-old boy believed to have been kidnapped by his biological mother, Holly Cranfield, and two unidentified men. Jack lived with his mother and father in the very apartment complex that is on fire at this time. Jack's father is away on business and is unavailable for comment at this time. They were last seen in a light blue *Holy Cross* rransport van entering the parking structure at *The Shops at 2000 Penn.* Any one having information on their possible whereabouts is asked to call 911."

Kirk picked up his telephone and dialed a number.

A woman answered the telephone, "Hello?"

"Hello, this is Kirk. We have a situation and need to make a change. We are following the Jack Gregory route."

The woman answered him, "We know and have taken care of it. Stay the course."

Kirk hung up the telephone. They pulled off of the highway onto White Pool Road to get some gas. Holly went into the gas station to use the restroom and get a drink. She was starting to feel very anxious and a headache was developing. She noticed that on the television on the front counter there was her and her son's picture being displayed along with the Amber alert story. Luckily there was nobody else in the store and the attendant had his back to the TV. When she returned to the car, she told Kirk, "They have my picture out on TV, and I think I heard them say something about road blocks."

Bill answered, "The same thing happened when I broke out."

"What do you mean 'broke out'?"

"That is what I call getting out of the system and being free."

"So how did you get past the road blocks?" Kirk asked.

"Well, I'm not sure. We were told by Henry's people to stay on course, and even though we went through a road block and they looked in our vehicle, nothing happened."

Holly asked, "Yes, but were you traveling with a child on a gurney hooked up to a respirator and feeding tubes? I'm sure that that will be a dead giveaway."

Bill nodded, "Yeah, I know that it doesn't make any sense, but I'm telling you, it will be handled. Henry has never lost a person yet."

Kirk looked at Holly and asked, "Are you feeling okay?"

"I'm just stressed, and I'm beginning to get a headache. Does it seem extra bright outside to you?"

Kirk asked, "Have you taken your meds yet today?"

"No, I didn't have time this morning, and now I can't find them. I think that I might have forgotten them. Maybe we should find a pharmacy."

Bill answered, "That would be a sure fire way to get caught. We can't let you get scanned. In fact, you are probably a bit feverish so you better not enter any more public buildings. The scanners will pick up your fever and alarms will sound."

As they continued on the road, the tension grew in the van. Holly felt increasingly anxious and her head was killing her. She tried to distract herself by focusing on Jack and tending to him, reading to him, and trying to sleep. Just outside of Hancock, Maryland, Bill started to slow the van and said, "Here we go." Holly looked up and peered out the front window to see flashing police lights and State Troopers standing out on the highway stopping cars. Her heart began to pound, and she felt her mouth go dry. As they pulled up to the officer, Bill rolled down his window. The Trooper put his head slightly in the window and looked back at Holly and Jack. He didn't say a word, but just looked across the car to his partner and nodded. They both waved their arms instructing Bill to continue on. As they pulled away from the check point, Holly couldn't hold back the tears. She felt such a tremendous sense of relief. She thought for sure that due to her husband's position, they were caught.

CHAPTER 10

THE RED CAMRY moved on in total silence for about five minutes.

"So, where are we going?" asked Eric.

Henry looked at Eric for a moment, then he looked at the driver, then back at James, seated behind him, then back at Eric.

"As soon as I found out . . .", Henry started, "What they were planning to do with my Biostrip invention, I realized that I had to prepare a way to get people out of bondage and prevent them from enslaving others. Luckily, due to the royalties that I am paid for the very thing that I am trying to destroy, I have nearly unlimited recourses. I went to work designing a new biostrip. A much smarter biostrip. This new biostrip is programmed to automatically update vaccination information, and to send out false physiological readings. It also changes the identity of the person in whom it is implanted."

Eric interrupted him, "Why not just take the damn thing out for good?"

Henry smiled, "We still have to live in this sick world Eric. We have to work, buy groceries, and send our children to school. We have to look just like everybody else." Henry looked over at the driver, "I am not alone in my efforts Eric. I have a lot of help, and some of it in very high places. Those who are the Insiders, who are behind all of this have enemies that they are unaware of. We have been very careful to not let on who they are. We have gone to great lengths even to look like we are at odds with them. This is a strategy that we learned from the Insiders. They will fund both sides of an issue, just to get and keep the debate going. If the issue is not discussed, then it is forgotten. They are expert at presenting a utopian-like solution to problems that really don't exist. So, thanks to some very enlightened people in high places we are able to do likewise. Do you recognize this gentleman driving for us Eric?"

Eric looked in the rear view mirror at the face of the driver. He hadn't even given him a second glance since they got in the car.

"Well, you do look a bit familiar, but I'm not sure."

"Eric", said Henry, "This is Dr. Calvin from the Center for Disease Control. You met him at the hospital."

Eric quickly looked in the mirror again for a better look.

"I don't understand. If Clare is with you, then why was she so afraid of you?"

"Because,", said Henry, "Clare has no idea that he is with us. This is why we have the mark."

Eric remembered the two dots on Clare's wrist. Clare had told him that he could know who he could trust by that. Clare never got close enough to Dr. Calvin to get a look at his wrist.

"Henry it has been fifteen minutes, we need to get rid of this vehicle," said Dr. Calvin as they pulled into the parking structure of City Creek Mall in downtown Salt Lake City. He put a baseball cap on before pulling up to the parking ticket machine, so that cameras could not pick up his face. He reached out and took the ticket from the machine. The arm went up, and they drove through. He parked the car and they went to work wiping it down to get rid of any finger prints. They then left the vehicle and went into the mall. They went to the food court and sat at a table. Henry pulled an envelope out of his coat pocket and handed it to Eric.

"Here are your instructions. We have to assume that you are being watched. We have safe biostrips, so we can easily disappear. You will have to do a bit more to disappear. Good luck, I will see you soon."

They each, except for Eric, got up from the table and left. Eric sat there feeling like he just realized that he was in school with no pants on. Eric opened the envelope and pulled out the paper. The first thing it said was, "Go to the nearest restroom and enter a stall before reading anymore." Eric put the envelope in his pocket and went to find a restroom. He entered a stall, pulled out the envelope and continued to read. "Memorize the rest of these instructions, and then flush this paper." Eric spent the next fifteen minutes memorizing the instructions, flushed the paper down the toilet, and left the stall. He looked around to make sure that he was alone. He made two cool compresses with paper towels. One he put on his wrist, and the other he put on the back of his neck. With the cool compresses in place he left the restroom. On his way out he took notice of the security camera and bioscanner located in the hallway just outside of the bathroom. Eric looked down at the floor and went directly to the mall map. He located the GNC store on the map and headed that way at a very quick pace. As he entered the GNC store, he removed his cool compresses and put them in the trash. He walked to the right back corner of the store and stood there looking at the products. A sales clerk approached him and asked if he could help him.

"I need to get rid of a fungus." Eric said.

The store clerk's face got serious.

He looked around, and then said, "You will need some of our Blue Algae ointment. Follow me, please."

The clerk led Eric to the register and pulled a tube of ointment from under the counter. The clerk handed the ointment to Eric.

"Go ahead and apply it now," the Clerk said.

Eric opened the tube and applied a thick blob of it to the back of his neck. It was very cold. Then he applied it to his wrist.

"Thank you," he said to the clerk.

"You will need to re-apply it every fifteen minutes," the clerk said.

Eric nodded and turned to leave the store, putting the tube of ointment into his pocket. Eric went to the closest mall map again, and located City Creek Dental. He quickly walked to the elevators. Before entering the elevator, he applied more cream to his wrist and neck. As Eric entered the elevator he noticed the security camera and bioscanner. He had never really given much thought to where all of these were when he was out in public. Again, Eric made a conscious effort to look down, keeping the back of his head toward the camera. Eric applied more cream just before entering the dental office. As Eric walked into the dental office he looked around. There was a woman with a child quietly playing with some toys at one end of the waiting room and a man reading a magazine, sitting just inside the door. The TV was on and there was something about an Amber alert in Maryland. In the background he could hear the sound of the dentist's drill and some muffled voices from one of the treatment rooms. Eric thought back to the last time he was in a dentist office. He didn't want to go, but Sarah had made the appointment for him and insisted that he keep it. It was uncomfortable to him to have stranger's hands in his mouth. He didn't like dentist offices.

"May I help you?" he heard the receptionist ask, snapping him back into the moment.

Eric approached the reception counter, and in a low voice said, "Somebody told me that a dentist might be able to help me with my headache."

The receptionist's smile left her face, and she looked very serious. "Where does your head hurt?" she asked.

"In the back of my head", replied Eric. The receptionist pushed a button unlocking the door that led back to the treatment area.

"Go through the door and take the second hallway on your left to room five."

Eric hesitated for just a second, then did as he was instructed. He walked passed a few treatment rooms on his way to room five. In each room there was a patient in a chair, but in only two they were actually being treated at that moment. Eric entered room five, which was empty, and sat down, or rather, reclined in the comfortable dentist chair. After nervously waiting for what seemed to be forever, but was actually only about five minutes, a man entered the room.

"My name is Dr. Rausch. I understand that you are having some trouble with your head."

Eric nodded. Dr. Rausch pulled out what looked like a car keyless entry transmitter and pointed it at the wall. He pushed a button. A hidden door in the wall opened up, and Dr. Rausch led Eric through it. They entered a cement hallway, not unlike the one at Henry's house. Eric wondered if the doctor was going to set off a bomb destroying the dentist office and incinerating all of the patients within. The door closed behind them as they walked down the hallway about fifty yards. On the wall, there was a keypad. Dr. Rausch reached up and keyed in a code. Another door opened up, and they walked through it entering what looked like an operating room. Dr. Rausch motioned to a chair for Eric to sit in, then went to an intercom on the wall and pushed a button. He then turned to Eric and said, "You are here to have your biostrip replaced. This will require a minor surgical procedure on your wrist, and a more complicated procedure on your neck. I am not a dentist, but a neurosurgeon. I assure you that this is a safe procedure, but it is not without some discomfort. What do you know about the biostrip?"

Eric thought back to what he had been told by Henry. "I know that it has two parts, I know that the part in the neck actually comes from a cockroach, and uses my nervous system to transmit my information picked up by the device in my wrist."

"Very good", said Dr. Rausch. "It is called a Host Transmitter or 'HT' for short, and is actually a hybrid organism that works synergistically with your body. Now we can't just go in and cut it out. First we will inject a fluorescent dye into your blood stream. This is quickly picked up by the HT. Then we entice the HT out of your body. We do that by making the environment in your body such that it stimulates the reproductive instincts in the HT. We will be raising your body temperature to 101 degrees Fahrenheit. You, of course, will be under anesthesia. We will also place pheromones by the incision, and we will have the lights off in the room. After about twenty-five minutes of your body temperature being that high, the HT will leave your body through the incision that we will make in the back of your neck. It will be visible because of the fluorescent dye, and we will retrieve it. We will then remove the pheromone from the surface of your skin, and with a syringe we will carefully place some sterile pheromone deep in the incision site. Then we will place a newly engineered HT at the incision site and the pheromone will entice it into your body. Once we have it in you, we will sew you up and allow your body temperature to drop back to normal. The biostrip in your wrist is an easy procedure. We simply remove the existing biostrip, and replace it with another. Are you ready to proceed?"

While Dr. Rausch was talking, Eric noticed three nurses entering the room and without speaking, they busily prepared everything. He was sickened by the thought of what was in him, but glad to be getting rid of it.

"Yes," Eric said.

Without hesitation one of the nurses came and handed Eric a gown, "Please go into that room there, and remove all of your clothes. Put the gown on so that it opens in the back, and then come back out here," the nurse instructed.

Eric did so, and when he came out of the changing room, he was escorted to the operating table in the center of the room. There was a computer console and other medical devices and monitors on a stand next to the table by his head.

Another nurse came to Eric's side, "Hello, my name is Sharon, and I will be administering your anesthesia. I'm going to do a quick biostrip scan to see if you have any allergies. Is that okay?"

Eric nodded.

Sharon waved a wand over Eric's wrist and pushed a few keys on the computer next to the operating table.

"Very good," she said. "When was the last time you had anything to eat?" Sharon asked Eric.

Eric hadn't realized it, but he had not had anything other than the drink at Henry's house since yesterday.

"I haven't eaten since yesterday", he replied.

"Very good."

Sharon had been busy getting ready to put an IV in Eric's arm.

"You are going to feel a little stick."

Eric winced a bit as she stuck the needle into the large vein on the soft part of his arm.

"Now, you may feel this anesthesia as it goes in. It will feel a bit cool."

Eric could feel the cool burn of the anesthesia, and almost immediately his head felt heavy, and his ears felt a bit clogged. He remembers seeing Sharon place an air mask over his mouth and nose, and in a far way voice say, "Just breathe deep Eric."

Eric woke up with a terrible pain in the back of his head and neck. He was confused and disoriented at first, and had to take a minute to try to recall where he was.

He heard a woman's voice, "Mr. Dunn, you are okay. You are just waking up from a surgical procedure. Do you have any pain?"

He tried to focus his eyes, and gather his thoughts.

Again, the woman said, "Do you have any pain, Mr. Dunn?"

Then he remembered he had entered the dentist office. That was the last clear memory that he could recall.

"Am I still in the dentist office?" he asked.

"You are in Dr. Rausch's surgical recovery room. We are right next to the dentist office. How do you feel?"

"Confused, and my head is killing me."

"As soon as you can sit up and drink some juice, I can give you something for your pain."

"What happened?" Eric asked.

"You had the organic part of your biostrip removed and your inorganic part replaced in your wrist."

Eric raised his arm up to see the bandage on his wrist. His brain fog was beginning to leave him, and he was starting to remember. *How long did that take, and how long have I been lying here?* The nurse was now standing at the side of the bed where Eric could see her. She was a middle aged woman with short brown hair very stylishly cut. She was wearing purple scrub bottoms and a white printed scrub top. She had a kind, very straight and white smile.

"The procedure only took about an hour, and you have been asleep for just about fifteen minutes. Do you feel like you can sit up and drink some juice?"

Eric nodded and the nurse pushed a button on the side rail which caused the top half of the bed to elevate. As soon as Eric was upright enough to drink, the bed stopped. She handed him a juice box with a straw sticking out of it.

"Just take small sips," she instructed him.

The juice was cool and sweet, and tasted very good to Eric.

"When you are ready, here are some Tylenol."

The nurse sat a small paper cup on the table next to Eric.

"How soon can I leave here?" Eric asked.

"Just as soon as you feel stable enough," she answered.

Eric picked up the cup with the pills in it and put them in his mouth. He washed them down with a couple of swigs of juice, then looked around the room. It was a small room that was not decorated at all. Stark white walls and tan carpet. But it was warm, and he felt safe.

"I feel okay", said Eric. "I think that I can stand up now."

Eric felt a little wobbly at first when he got up, but after a couple of seconds he was fine.

"You will have to change your dressing twice per day," the nurse told Eric while handing him a box of flesh color two inch square adhesive bandages. She then led him to an exit door, and held it open for him.

She said "Goodbye," with a smile.

Eric found himself in a long, narrow hallway with a green exit sign above the door at the end of the hallway to his right. To his left, the hallway went on passed three other doors, then took a turn to the right. Eric went toward the exit sign. He tried to go over in his mind the instructions that he had memorized. *What next?* he thought to himself. As he pushed through the door, he found himself back in the mall. Then it dawned on him what he was supposed to do next. He quickly found a mall map and oriented himself to where he was. He found his way to the exit onto South Temple Street and to the nearest commuter train stop.

As he entered the train, he waved his wrist over the bioscanner to pay the fare and wondered why that was safe to do.

Won't they now be able to track me? he wondered. As Eric rode west toward the airport, he looked around at all of the people, thinking how blind everyone is, and how blind he was. He felt empowered for the first time in his life. Eric exited the train at the airport and went to the Budget car rental desk. He felt his heart begin to race when he saw a TSA guard standing by the car rental desk.

The clerk smiled and asked, "Do you have a reservation?"

"Yes," Eric answered with his heart pounding, knowing that the next question would be, "What name is the reservation in?"

Instead, the clerk asked Eric to scan his biostrip. Eric hesitated for a moment. The TSA guard seemed to increase his focus on Eric. He thought that he was caught for sure. Homeland Security was obviously looking for him, and had TSA on high alert. Hesitantly, he waved his wrist over the bioscanner.

The clerk looked at his computer, and said, "I'm sorry, Mr. Chandler, I know that you reserved a compact car but we are all out. I will have to upgrade you to a full size, but I will give you the compact price."

Eric just stood and stared at the clerk. He couldn't believe what he was hearing. The TSA guard seemed to relax also.

"Thank you!" Eric blurted out.

"Okay, everything is taken care of with your bioscan. Just wait for our shuttle outside and they will take you to your car."

CHAPTER 11

CLARE GOT UP from her chair and suggested that Sarah get some rest.

"You must be exhausted," she said. "You gave birth yesterday, and were abducted today. I don't know too many women who could handle such extreme situations. You are very strong, Sarah."

Clare looked at Sarah with a warm look on her face. She turned and left the room. Again, Sarah was left to think. She wasn't feeling the same anger anymore that she had experienced earlier. Instead, she was feeling understanding toward Clare and her husband. *Clare*, she thought, *She is a very kind woman for a criminal.* Sarah smiled to herself. *What was it about Clare*, she thought, *that made her so endearing?*

Sarah sat in silence feeding Eric, Jr. for quite a while. The next thing she knew, she was waking up to Eric, Jr.'s crying. She quickly went to the bassinet, thinking that she didn't remember putting him down. She turned him over to pick him up, but when she turned him toward her, she jumped back with a terrible scream. Eric, Jr.'s face had changed. His eyes were too big for his head, and his skin didn't look young anymore, it looked old. Sarah started to call for help.

"Help! Help!" she kept calling out and finally her calls woke her up.

She looked around the room confused for a second, but then she remembered. She looked down at Eric, Jr. who was asleep in her arms, and raised him up to give him a kiss on the forehead. The door opened, and Clare came in.

"Are you okay?" Clare asked.

"Yes," said Sarah looking at Clare's eyes. *Those are the eyes that I saw on Eric, Jr. in my dream.*, she thought to herself. "I just had a bad dream, Sarah said to Clare"

Clare smiled, "Do you need anything?"

"No, I think I am fine," Sarah replied.

As Clare turned to leave, Sarah called out to her, "Clare?"

Clare turned around.

"You can hold Eric, Jr. now if you want."

Clare looked shocked. She walked over to Sarah and softly said "thank you" as she leaned down to take him out of Sarah's arms. Clare sat down in the other chair and softly bounced Eric, Jr. up and down while she sang to him.

"I love you, you love me, we are a happy family."

"Clare?" Sarah asked.

Clare looked up at Sarah, "Hmm?"

Clare had a soft, kind smile on her face, the kind of smile that Sarah had seen many times in photos of herself.

"Do you have any children?"

Clare looked down at Eric, Jr. and was quiet. After about a minute, Clare said, "Yes. I had a child. She was taken from me."

Sarah's heart began to pound.

"What happened?" Sarah asked, fully anticipating the answer.

Clare didn't answer for quite some time. She just stared at Sarah with a longing in her tear-filled eyes. Softly, she said, "The vaccinations took her from me," as her tears finally broke loose of her lower eyelid and ran down her face. Sarah didn't know what to say. This was not exactly the answer that she thought she would get. Clare's voice, her smile, the feeling that Sarah had when Clare was there, coupled with the dream that Sarah had, all gave Sarah the impression that *maybe, just maybe* Clare was her mother. Now she kind of felt silly for thinking that.

"Clare", Sarah said with warmth in her voice that had not been there before, "I am sorry for your loss. I can't imagine what it would be like to not be able to see and hold and love my baby. I understand why you are doing what you are doing, but please understand that I fear losing my baby if I get him vaccinated, and if I don't. I feel like I am stuck. You can be strong; you do not have anything to lose anymore. I can't just make that decision based on your word alone."

Clare didn't answer her, she just looked down at Eric, Jr., who was sleeping in her arms. She hummed softly to him. Sarah watched Clare as she heldher son with such love and warmth. She could feel Clare's love for her son and that made Sarah love Clare. She wasn't angry or scared anymore. She felt safe.

Clare looked up at Sarah and said, "I said that the vaccines took my daughter from me, but I didn't say that she had died. I want you to know that I have more to lose than you think. When my daughter was an infant, I made the decision to not have her vaccinated."

Sarah listened intently, her heart now beginning to race again. "My husband didn't see things the way that I did, and because of the laws that had been put into place he was able to divorce me and totally take away all of my parental rights. I lost my daughter, knowing that she would most likely be raised by someone else and never know that I love her. In prison, I was sterilized against my will because the state deemed me an unfit mother. Now, I run the risk of losing my daughter, who I am talking with for the first time since she was taken from me, and my grandson."

Sarah's tears flowed freely now as she realized that she was right. Clare is her mother. Sarah just sat and sobbed for a few minutes.

"I'm so sorry that you had to grow up without me, Sarah" Clare said. "I have thought of you always and have watched you from a distance longing for the day when I could be in your life. I had to be careful though, because I didn't know how you would react. I didn't want to wind up in prison again."

Sarah wiped the tears from her face, and looked at Clare.

"I am so sorry for what you have gone through. I have longed to know you, and have wondered about you."

"Are you disappointed that I'm not a bag lady who is missing two teeth?" Clare said through a smile.

Sarah laughed, "No, I just said those things because I was angry. Can I ask you something?"

"Sure, anything," Clare answered. "I was just wondering, how long were you in prison, and how did you become a labor and delivery nurse with your record?"

"I was in prison for three years. While I was in prison, I was told about a man that had designed a way to help people be free of the government oppression. So when I got out, I went looking for him. You will meet him later today. That is who Eric is with right now. His name is Henry, and he is the one who invented the biostrip that they use to enslave us. It is really our shackle. My name is not really Clare. My real name is Rose. But when Henry gave me a new biostrip, he also gave me a new identity. That allowed me to go to school and get an education. That is why you will not be caught, because you are not on your own as I was."

Sarah didn't respond to what Clare said, but instead asked, "So when you got out of prison, I was three years old. Did you try to find me, then?"

Clare nodded, "I did. But you have to understand, my parental rights were totally taken away. All of your records were closed to me, and I was forbidden from having any contact with you. I couldn't go to the county recorder and ask for birth records. I did go back to where we lived when you were born, but you had moved. I was at a dead end, and had no hope of finding you until I met Henry. I explained my situation to him, and not only did he help me get free, he also found you for me. I have watched you from afar, all the time longing to speak to you and tell you who I am. Do you remember your senior ball?"

Sarah gave Clare a puzzled look.

"I was there Sarah. I worked with the photographer that took your pictures."

Clare reached into her pocket, took out a photograph and handed it to Sarah. "I have carried this with me since then. That was the closest that I ever got to you physically." Sarah stared at the photograph and tears began to flow again.

"That's not fair," she said, "All of my friends were able to go to the dance without their parents there spying on them, but not me."

Sarah got up, walked over to Clare, bent down and put her arms around her shoulders.

"I have waited too long to hug you," she said.

"I love you, Sarah" said Clare.

"So what is going to happen now?" Sarah asked.

"We are heading to Evanston, Wyoming. There we will meet up with Eric and go to a local safe house. At the safe house, if you are willing, you and Eric, Jr. will be implanted with the new biostrip."

Sarah's heart sank. She was afraid of Eric, Jr. being implanted with the legal biostrip, let alone an illegal one.

"What about my husband? Won't he also be implanted?" Sarah asked.

"Well," Clare replied, I believe that he will have already been implanted before he gets here. But if he hasn't, than, yes he will also be implanted."

Clare knew that he had already been implanted, but she didn't want to make Sarah feel like she was being painted into a corner.

"How soon will we be in Evanston?" asked Sarah.

"Let me check," Clare said handing Eric, Jr. back to Sarah. She opened the door and stepped halfway out. "How soon till we reach Evanston, Doug?" she said to someone outside the room.

"Ten minutes," Sarah heard a man's voice reply.

Clare tuned and looked at Sarah with a smile, "Just ten more minutes," she said.

"I heard," said Sarah.

"Who is Doug?"

"Doug is my husband and your step-father. You will meet him in ten minutes. I think that you will really like him."

Sarah didn't respond. She just smiled and looked at Eric, Jr. *This is crazy!* she thought to herself. *Suddenly I have living parents again. I was just feeling sorry for myself because my parents were gone, and now I have parents again.* But Sarah knew that she would not have parents if she chose not to "escape" as Clare called it. She knew that this could very well be the first and last time that she would see her Mom, because she could not put her at risk if she decided to stay in the system.

CHAPTER 12

"**D**IRECTOR, THIS IS the pilot speaking, we will be landing in thirty minutes. Please prepare yourself for landing," a male voice said over the speaker system in the cabin of the plane that Director Harrison and agent Cranfield were on.

The director shut down her computer system, turned her chair back to the front of the plane, and fastened her seatbelt. Allen just put on his seat belt. After landing, they exited the plane and were met by two agents from the Salt Lake division.

"Director Harrison, I am Agent Tom Milchen, and this is Agent Sean Barry. We have information about Agent Cranfield's wife."

"Wait until we are in the car," the director said abruptly.

After they were settled in the car and moving toward the exit, the Director said, "Let's hear what you have got."

"Our team followed the light blue medical transport van to *The Shops at 2000 Penn*. The van entered the parking garage and we placed vehicles at each exit. They have not left the garage."

"How long ago was that?" she asked.

"An hour ago, Ma'am."

"Get teams in that garage right now looking for that van. I will be willing to bet that they don't find it. I also want traffic cam shots of every exit of that parking garage. Get the license plate and registration information of every van that left that garage after they entered it. Let's also get the bioscan of the driver of that van as he took his parking ticket, and cross reference that with the bioscan of any other van leaving the garage and the registrations."

"Why only vans?" Milchen asked.

"Mrs. Cranfield is traveling with a son who requires quite a bit of medical equipment. I'm sure that they can't travel with all that in a Prius," Harrington said sarcastically.

"Ma'am", Milchen said, "There is one more thing that you need to know. There was an explosion and fire at the Cranfield's apartment building just after Mrs. Cranfield left."

"What do we know about the fire?" asked the Director.

"We know that it was started by a small explosion in the Cranfield's apartment, Ma'am."

"Were we able to recover the CI recording?" the Director asked.

"No Ma'am, the box was there, but the drive had been removed and we only found a small piece of it in the rubble."

Allen spoke up, "Any word yet on the guards at my Da-," he stopped himself before saying the word, "Professor Cranfield's residence?"

The Director felt that he was changing the subject, but didn't say anything. Agent Milchen was on the phone, so agent Barry answered, "Just that we located the guard residence, Sir, and it was vacated. We have a team working that scene now."

Allen was surprised by being called Sir.

He said, "We are going there now, correct?"

"Yes sir, we will be there in about fifteen minutes."

The Director's telephone rang, and she answered it.

"Director Henderson."

A female voice on the other end spoke up, "Ma'am, we have a report of a missing woman and her newborn child from the Barack Obama Medical Center."

"How long have they been missing?" she asked.

"About an hour, Ma'am."

"Who is our contact there?" the Director asked.

"Dr. Bernstein, Ma'am."

"Good, can you patch me through to him?"

"Yes Ma'am, hold one minute please."

While she was on hold she told Agent Barry, who was driving, to change course and head to the medical center first.

"What's up?" Allen asked.

The Director told him about the missing woman, and in the middle of telling him she heard the female agent on the phone say, "Director Henderson, I have Dr. Bernstein on the line for you, Ma'am."

"Thank you," she said, "Dr. Bernstein, this is Director Henderson with Homeland Security. What can you tell me about the woman and child that are missing?"

Dr. Bernstein spoke up, "Her name is Laura Dunn. She gave birth early this morning. Dr. Calvin, of the CDC and I spoke with her husband after their child was born. We had heard of a possible plot to remove a child from our facility to avoid vaccinations. We spoke to all the new fathers. We are fairly certain that Mr. Dunn was truthful with us."

"What other new fathers did you speak with?" Director Henderson asked.

"Well, none; the only other new father, well officially, anyway, didn't even make it to the hospital with his wife. They were all killed in a car accident on their way here."

"I see", said Henderson, "I am on my way there. I want to meet with you and Dr. Calvin. I also want video of your facility to include elevators and parking structure. Also look for bioscans of Laura Dunn."

"Will do" he replied.

The Director hung up the telephone. Director Henderson told Milchen to get everything that he could on Laura and Eric Dunn. He got on his laptop and went to work on that.

"It looks like your Dad is not only taking your wife and son, but someone else too." she said to Allen. "I have been working on this terrorist ring for two years, and now I am going to crush it." she said to no one in particular, with a victorious air about her.

Allen just nodded in silence.

"Ma'am?" Milchen said. "We have information on the Dunns. Mr. Dunn is really a nobody, but his wife is a different story. Her birth mother is Rose Brady. When Sarah was born, she tried to prevent her vaccination and implantation. Sarah's father turned her in and divorced her. Rose was sentenced to ten years, and was released on parole after serving three years. Two months into her parole, she disappeared. There has never been another bioscan picked up from her since then."

"Do we have a photograph of Rose Brady?" asked the Director.

"Yes ma'am . . . We have her mug shots."

"I want a forensic artist's drawing of what she is likely to look like now, and have it sent to my cell phone ASAP."

Milchen didn't say anything, but went right to work on getting what she asked for. They arrived at the hospital, and were met at the entrance by Doctors Bernstein and Calvin. They reached out to shake the Director's hand, and before they could say anything she ordered, "Do not say a word until we are in a secure location."

They walked through the main entrance of the hospital in silence, and entered an elevator. Dr. Bernstein used a key to open a panel inside the elevator which exposed a button for B3, a third level basement that did not have a button on the main panel. Her pushed the button and held it down. A male voice came over the loud speaker, "Good morning Dr. Bernstein. I have a positive bioscan for you, Dr. Calvin, Alice Henderson, Allen Cranfield, Tom Milchen, and Sean Barry. Is that correct Doctor?"

Dr. Bernstein looked around at everybody in the elevator and said, "Yes, that is correct."

The elevator began to drop. Within a few seconds the elevator doors opened, and they all exited following Dr. Bernstein to a large boardroom. They all sat around the table and Dr. Bernstein closed the door and after passing his wrist over the bioscanner on the wall, he entered a code into a key pad next to the bioscanner and the glass wall went opaque.

"We are secure" he said.

"Good" said the Director. "I need to know everything that happened with the Dunns when they were here."

"Well," said Dr. Bernstein, "We first found Mr. Dunn in the cafeteria where he was talking with our head labor and delivery nurse."

"About what?" the director asked.

"Well, he said that she was giving him some 'first time father' advice."

The Director turned and looked at Dr. Calvin who was sitting across the table from her, with his sunglasses on and silently listening.

"Were you there Dr. Calvin?" she asked.

"Yes I was," he answered.

"Dr. Bernstein, may we dim the lights for Dr. Calvin please?" the Director asked.

Dr. Bernstein got up and went to the wall switch and dimmed the lights a bit. Dr. Calvin removed his sunglasses. Allen figured that he had some sort of pigmentation problem causing him to be photophobic.

"Gentlemen", the Director spoke up, "What I am about to reveal to you is crypto top secret. It requires that we do a bioscan of each of you to verify your security clearance."

She looked over at Dr. Calvin and nodded. He quietly looked at each individual in the room for just a few seconds, and then, after looking at each one he turned to the Director and nodded.

"Very good", she said. "Dr. Calvin, is one of many human bioscanners. He has been kept off of any immunosuppressive drugs, and his body temperature has been kept at its biologically normal 98.2 to 99.0 degree range. Consequently, the exogenous tissue that has been implanted in his nervous system has dominated his sensory system allowing him to receive information from any individual's bioscanner. We have not made this information public, and we desire it to stay that way. It is possible for us to use individuals such as Dr. Calvin to determine if someone is being truthful or not. So Dr. Calvin, when you spoke with Mr. Dunn, was he in fact being truthful?"

Dr. Calvin looked at the Director for some time, in silence. The Director looked back. Everybody else in the room could feel this connection between Dr. Calvin and the Director, but nobody said anything. Finally, after what seemed like five minutes, Dr. Calvin quietly and simply said, "Yes."

The Director looked up at the top of the wall behind Dr. Calvin, and took in a deep breath. She let it out with a sigh as she sat back in her chair.

"Well then, it seems as though Dr. Cranfield has developed a way to mask the signals being emitted by the bioscanner, or at least mute them a bit. You say you spoke with him in the cafeteria, correct?"

Dr. Bernstein answered, "Yes."

"Do we have any security cameras in the cafeteria?" she asked.

"Yes we do," said Dr. Bernstein, "I will pull them up right now and play them on the monitor right over there."

He pointed to the opposite end of the room where a large flat panel HD monitor was mounted on the wall. He pulled out a lap top computer from a compartment under the table and began entering information. Within a minute the monitor turned on and was playing video footage of the cafeteria. They could see Eric and Clare sitting at a table together. Clare's back was to Dr.'s Bernstein and Calvin. The camera was to Clare's left.

"Do we have audio?" the Director asked.

"No ma'am. The cafeteria is too large and at times very crowded. We felt that audio would be unproductive." Dr. Bernstein answered.

They saw Clare give Eric the two pills that he took and the herb tea.

"There it is," said the Director matter of factly. "She gave him something to mute his biotransmissions and to regulate his vitals."

Just then, the Director's phone sounded a message notice. She opened the message to see an artist rendition of what they think Rose Brady would look like today. She looked up at the screen as Clare was walking out of the cafeteria, and said in a commanding tone, "Pause right there!"

She looked at the screen and then back at the picture a few times.

"Gentlemen", she said, pointing at the monitor, "Meet our long lost Rose Brady. What time did Mrs. Dunn go missing?"

Dr. Bernstein spoke up, "About 10:30 this morning."

"Do we have video of a parking structure that shows her leaving?"

"No," said Dr. Bernstein. "That's what is so strange. We don't know how she got out of the building."

There was silence in the room for a moment and then Allen spoke up. "Maybe they carried her out in something."

"Yeah, that's likely", said Milchen in a sarcastic tone. "A lady with her baby, maybe they put them in a big box."

"Wait a minute", said the Director, I think that Agent Cranfield is on to something. Do you have video of the morgue exit?"

"Yes" said Bernstein.

"Pull up any video from 10:00 A.M. to 11:00 A.M.."

Dr. Bernstein went to work on his keyboard punching keys, and a few moments later he said, "Here it is, beginning at 10 A.M. this morning."

"Go ahead a fast forward at four times normal speed", the Director said.

He pushed a button and the video began to move fast.

"Stop!" she said.

He pushed a button and the picture froze.

"Go back a bit."

He pushed another button and the picture started moving backward. Suddenly they saw on the screen a lady and a man pushing a gurney out with a body bag on top of it, and putting the body bag into a black hearse.

"Check with the morgue and see if they had a pick up today."

Dr. Bernstein got on his computer and after a minute said, "No. There is no pick up on record."

"Let's run the plates on that hearse and get the bioscan information off the driver when he exited the garage," the director ordered Milchen. "Good thinking Allen", she said. "What is the time stamp on this frame?" she asked Dr. Bernstein.

"10:37 A.M.," he replied.

"Okay," she said, "It is now 12:40 P.M.. I want road blocks on all major highways in a two hundred mile radius from here and a code red at the airport. Make sure that the TSA has information on the driver and Laura Dunn. We better be on the look out for Eric Dunn, also."

Cranfield got on his phone to call it in, "Hello, State Police?" Allen said into his telephone. "Good, this is Agent Allen Cranfield with the Department of Homeland Security. We need a two hundred mile radius from Salt Lake City lockdown on all major highways. My security clearance code should be enough authorization. You can verify it with our office in DC. My code is two, seven, niner, zero, delta, alpha, eight, foxtrot, echo. We need all vehicles scanned for a Laura and or Eric Dunn. If you find either one, detain them and contact me at the number that I am calling you from." He listened for a moment and then said, "Yes, that is correct. Thank you."

He hung up his phone, and dialed another number to reach the TSA. After a few seconds he said, "Hello, this is Agent Allen Cranfield with Homeland Security, I need the supervisor on duty." He waited for a moment then began to speak again, "This is agent Allen Cranfield with Homeland Security, my authorization code is two, seven, niner, zero, delta, alpha, eight, foxtrot, echo . . . I need Salt Lake International Airport security raised to code red . . . Looking for Laura and Eric Dunn, and," he looked over at Milchen who held up his cell phone for Allen to read, "Joel Thorne. They are to be detained and held for me. You can reach me at this number. Thank you."

He hung up the phone.

"Let's get over to Dr. Cranfield's place," the Director said.

As they arrived at his Dad's house, Allen was shocked at the devastation. There was nothing left of the house but a hole in the ground. They were met by two other agents who had been there for a while investigating.

"We have not been able to find evidence of anything but an explosion caused by a gas leak, Ma'am," one of the agents said.

They started to look around at the scene. Allen's phone rang.

"Hello, this is Agent Cranfield," he said after pushing the green button on his phone. He listened for a moment, and then said, "Very good. Let's get an A.P.B. out on that vehicle and its owner."

He hung up his phone then walked over to the Director who was standing in the lowest part of the crater, looking around at the dirt and debris.

"They've got some surveillance camera footage of the outside of the other building that burned down. There were three men that left that building just prior to the fire. They have been identified as Dr. Cranfield, Eric Dunn and James White. They got into a red Toyota Camry. They got a plate on the vehicle, and are putting out an A.P.B. on the vehicle, its owner, and the three men."

"So, the question is, how did they get from here to there without being seen?" the Director asked.

"An underground tunnel," said Allen.

"My Dad had nearly unlimited recourses, and with his paranoia, I would not put that past him."

"Then why don't we see any evidence of a tunnel?" asked the Director.

"It has got to be deeper than this" said Allen.

"Let's get a back hoe in her and dig this baby out. I bet we find a tunnel."

"Okay. Call it in," said Director Henderson as they climbed up out of the hole. "It's getting late, and I want to get settled into our hotel. Then we can get over to the Salt Lake Office of Homeland Security and have a briefing with everybody. We should be able to wrap this all up by tomorrow morning."

They climbed in their vehicle and headed to the Grand America Hotel in downtown Salt Lake City, which was one block from the Homeland Security office.

CHAPTER 13

THE SHUTTLE DROPPED Eric off in a parking lot. Eric looked at his paperwork, which had "H14" written in red and circled. He found parking stall H14. In it was a red Buick Verano. He got in the car and started it up. He looked around in the car and admired its nice interior. Chocolate colored leather, heated and cooled seats, digital display, stereo controls on the steering wheel, cruise control, power locks and windows, and a six CD stereo with Bluetooth capability. Eric had never driven a car this nice. He drove out of the parking lot and headed for I-15 northbound. He didn't know where he was going, he just knew that he was told to head north. He looked at his watch; it was 11:45 A.M.. His cell phone began to ring. He answered it.

"Hello."

"Eric, this is Henry. I am going to connect you with Sarah for a quick minute so that you can put her mind at ease a bit. Hold just a second."

Eric heard a clock, then silence, then a few seconds later he heard Sarah's voice.

"Hello?"

It was good to hear her voice. He told her what he could, but knew that he didn't have much time. He told her that he would see her soon and fill her in on everything. Then the phone went dead. Eric sat there for a minute and cried as he thought of his poor wife and new baby with strangers somewhere. He longed to be with them. He started the car and began to drive north. After thirty-five minutes on the highway, Eric passed through Ogden, Utah and he started to look for Exit 342. He exited I-15, and pulled off the road onto the shoulder and waited. This was as far as his instructions went. His head was starting to hurt again, so he took a couple more Tylenol then lied his seat back to try to relax. He was awakened by a phone ringing over the stereo speakers. He looked at the digital display and it read *Incoming call*. He looked around on his steering wheel for a button to push to answer, but he couldn't find one. Then he looked back at the digital display, and read under the words incoming call the words, *say answer to answer, ignore to ignore.*

"Answer!" he blurted out after the fifth ring. The ringing stopped, and he could hear someone breathing over the car speaker system.

"Hello?" he said.

"Hello, Eric?" a male voice came back over the speakers.

"Yes, who is this?"

"Eric, this is Henry."

Eric was relieved to hear his voice.

"Hi Henry, I was hoping to hear from you soon. Where am I going?"

"I will get to that in a moment," Henry said, "First, I need to know where you are right now."

"I did exactly was the instructions said, I got off on exit 342, parked on the side of the road and waited," he said.

Henry said, "Go east on State Highway 104, then turn right on 1100 West. Go to the round–bout and take the first right. About a quarter mile down the road, you will come to a little restaurant called Cactus Reds. I need you to just pull into the parking lot and park. I will call you back in about five minutes."

"Ok, will do," Eric replied.

The phone went dead.

Eric pulled into the parking lot of Cactus Reds diner, and parked in the most remotespot he could find away from other cars. He left the car running, and waited. He was wondering what his next move would be. Maybe there was another friend of Henry's here that was going to take him the rest of the way. He was really starting to wonder about Laura and Eric, Jr. He couldn't wait to see them again. The phone rang.

"Answer" he said. "Hello."

"Who is this?" he heard Henry ask.

Before he could give an answer, he heard his own voice in his head say, "Tom Chandler."

"What?" Eric said out loud.

"Give me the answer that you heard in your head," Henry said.

"Tom Chandler," Eric answered.

"Excellent," said Henry, "Your new biostrip has some features that I need to make you aware of. First of all, we removed the exogenous organism that was in your brainstem and added a new one. This one will not transmit your biological information as the other one did, but instead will transmit pre-programmed information. It also has a GPS capability that allows your identity to change depending on your location. In Utah, you are Tom Chandler. In Wyoming you will be someone else, and if you are scanned, it will read the information that we want it to read. The reason that you heard your voice in your head say Tom Chandler, is because by me asking 'who is this?', it triggered the organism to stimulate your primary auditory cortex as well as your primary speech cortex, and you heard yourself say your new name. Wherever you are, you can ask yourself, 'Who am I?' When we speak to ourselves in our heads, we stimulate those same regions of the brain that we stimulate when we actually speak and hear the words. Therefore, by asking this question, you will cause a response that you will hear in your head. Where are you from?" Henry asked.

Eric heard his own voice in his head say, "Wichita, Kansas.".

He responded out loud to Henry, "Wichita".".

Henry chuckled a bit because he could hear the awe in Eric's voice.

"Whatever you need to know about the person that you are is accessible simply by the question being asked by you or someone else. I needed to go over this with you before you went any further;before you began interacting with too many people. Do you have any questions?"

"Well if I do," Eric replied, "I guess that I will hear the answer in my head."

Henry laughed.

"One other thing that you need to know Eric, or I should say Tom; You will also be able to know the regional name of anybody else fitted with one of these new organisms. So when you are within ten yards of someone, you will hear your voice say a name when you look at them, then you will know that they are one of us."

"Well, that will definitely take some getting use to," Eric replied. "So where do I go from here?"

"I want you to travel east toward Cheyenne, Wyoming. When you get to Evanston, take exit 5 and turn left to go to McDonald's. When you get to McDonald's you will see a large gray and black RV with Arizona plates. Knock on the door and when answered you should hear your voice inside your head tell you the name of the person answering. They have your wife and son with them."

"I have a few other questions," Eric said.

"Go ahead," said Henry.

"What about my job, my apartment, and money?"

"Excellent questions", replied Henry. "You need to know that Eric Dunn no longer exists. You have a new identity now, and each time that you change states. I have the advantage of knowing the programs that run the biostrips. I set them up, and when I realized what they were going to do with them I created a secure back door entry for me to install my algorithms allowing for the new biostrips to work. In 2011 and 2012, the world economy took a big hit. This was no mistake, but it was planned. This allowed the government to create even more national debt with the bail-outs. Remember what I told you about how people will give up freedom for a cause?"

"Yes," said Eric.

"Well, following that economic hit, the economy made a small rebound while the administration spent an unprecedented amount of money driving our national debt higher than ever imagined. They also printed trillions of dollars that had no precious metals to back it. This caused the collapse of the dollar, and it was no longer recognized as the international currency. In late 2014, the United States of America declared bankruptcy. This created a threat, thereby opening the door to get the American people to gladly give up their sovereign currency, and the freedom that it brought, for the international currency credit. Europe was already poised for this, and other developed nations gladly followed. Third world countries had no choice but to join this movement, or be broke and have no way to trade internationally. Please understand, the ICC is not a real thing. There is nothing tangible about them, they are just a bunch of 1's and 0's on a computer. This was just another way to ensure our bondage, because you have to have the biostrip to receive and use your ICC. Well, again, my inside knowledge allowed me to create an algorithm that ensures that wherever you are, you have plenty of ICC. You don't have to worry about money. All that I ask, is that you stand ready to help others who may be trying to get out of bondage. You are not obligated. You are free to choose. If you want to relocate, and find employment doing what you have always done, you can do just that. Each of your identities has a built in curriculum vite that you can use to find employment. When you decide where you want to stay, you just need to call me and say that you want to lock in. I will then make that your permanent identity that will stay with you no matter where you go."

"Wow!" said Eric. "I guess that you have thought of everything. So, what do I do when I meet up with Laura?"

"Just go, and the people that she is with will give you more instructions."

"Thank you," Eric said, "I guess that I will talk to you later, or will I be seeing you later at all?"

"I will be seeing you later today. Drive safe. Goodbye," Henry said.

"Good bye", replied Eric, and the phone went dead.

Eric sat there in silence for a few minutes trying to take this all in. He wondered how Laura was going to take all of this. *Laura*, he thought, *I am just a little over an hour from being with her and Eric, Jr.* He started the car and headed for Evanston. For the next hour and twenty minutes he thought about what he and Laura would do now. Where would they live? Would they stay in one place? Would they live by family? *Family!?* Eric thought. *What about my parents?* He hadn't thought of that before now. How could he just disappear? His parents finally have a grandson, and now they would never see him. He started to get a bit choked up thinking of the possibility of never seeing his parents again. *I don't know if I can do that,* he thought. Then he remembered that he was doing all of this for his son. Was he willing to give up his son's freedom for the opportunity to see his parents? He decided then that he could never turn back. He spent the rest of his drive reminiscing about his childhood, and in essence, saying goodbye to his parents. It was a very emotional ride as he realized that he had seen them for the last time.

CHAPTER 14

HOLLY AWOKE TO the sound of a telephone ringing. She had finally dozed off and had slept for about an hour. She was lying down across the bench that she was sitting on. She didn't move, but just lied there and watched Jack while she listened to Kirk on the telephone.

"Hello", he said, "Oh, hello, Henry . . . This is Kirk."

There was a pause.

"We are almost to the Pennsylvania Turnpike."

Again he paused.

"Okay, 149. I got it. Then what?"

He listened for the answer.

"Okay, I got it. Goodbye."

He hung up the telephone. He turned to Bill and said, "We need to get off at exit 149, Lighthouse Road, there will be a large black and gray RV with Florida plates. We need to make contact there."

"What is going on?" Holly sat up while she asked that. Kirk turned around in his seat a bit.

"Henry only said that we need to make contact, he didn't tell me more than that."

"How long was I asleep?" she asked.

"A bit less than an hour, I guess," answered Kirk. "We stopped for gas, and you didn't even flinch."

One of Jacks alarms went off and Holly went to work quickly suctioning out his airway. She then prepared some food for him by hooking up a bottle of his nutrient drink to a syringe with a tube. She then hooked up the other end of the tube to his feeding port. She softly caressed Jack's forehead and quietly sang to him as she slowly pushed the food through the tube. She stopped singing and looked up at Kirk, "They must have made our vehicle." She said, "I bet that Henry wants us to get rid of this one."

Kirk burst out in laughter. "Made our vehicle! Where did you get that phrase? *Law and Order, SVU?*"

Holly smiled, "Well, you know what I mean."

"Yeah, I know what you mean. That could be the case. Let's just get there and find out."

"Well, we will find out very soon", said Bill, "Here is our exit."

They turned off of the exit and got to the end of the off-ramp. They looked to the right, and could see the RV parked on the shoulder. They pulled up behind the RV and stopped. Kirk got out of the van and walked up to the RV. Holly watched as he knocked on the RV door. She saw the door open and heard Kirk talking. He reached his hand out and shook hands with whoever it was that opened the door. Holly could not see who Kirk was talking to. She saw Kirk nodding his head, then he turned to his right to look down the road behind him and pointed. He then turned back to the person in the RV. Smiling he nodded and waved as he started to walk back to the van.

He climbed inside, and said to Bill, "We are going to follow the RV down this road to the right about a quarter mile, then we will take a left fork off this road onto a long driveway to a little farm house down here a bit."

"Okay," said Bill and he put it in drive.

"How do we know that we can trust them?" Holly asked.

Kirk turned to her and said, "It is difficult to explain, but when you get your new biostrip, you will understand."

"I need to get a new biostrip?" asked Holly.

"I thought the idea was to be free of the biostrip."

"The idea is to be free," Kirk replied, "But we need a biostrip to function and stay free."

"So," said Holly, "How and when do I get a new biostrip?"

"Well," said Kirk, "Mrs. Morrison, she is the lady in the RV, tells me that they are scanning everyone in vans on all highways just after the state line, so the when is right now. I will let the doctor explain the how."

"What!?" exclaimed Holly.

"I am going to get one right now?"

"We can't very well cross the state line with your current biostrip, can we?" asked Kirk.

They pulled up to the little farm house and got out of the van. Both Kirk and Bill came around to the back of the van to get Jack out. Mrs. Morrison, a tall stout woman in her mid-fifties wearing a flowered dress and an apron as though she had just dropped what she was doing in the kitchen to drive down to the highway, came from her RV over to Holly.

"You must be Holly," she said.

Holly put her hand out to shake hands, but Mrs. Morrison went right passed her hand and gave Holly a big hug. Holly felt the strength of Mrs. Morrison and thought how farm living had made her that strong.

"You are such a brave woman," said Mrs. Morrison.

"Thank you ma'am, but I don't feel very brave."

"Call me Marge, please. You are too brave, bringing your son out of bondage all on your own, especially with your husband being who he is and all."

Holly was surprised by the amount of information that Mrs. Morrison had. Kirk and Bill were pushing Jack in his bed into the farm house, and Mrs. Morrison was walking toward the house with a stout arm around Holly's shoulders. Holly felt her genuine warmth, but was a little off balance by it all. They entered the small farm house and Holly was hit by the warmth and smell of fresh cooked food and preserves that undoubtedly had been prepared in the kitchen daily for years. The house was not fancy, but it was clean and tidy. The wood floor creaked a bit when walked on, and there were rugs instead of wall-to-wall carpet. In the living room there was a pot belly stove that was emitting warmth that could be felt across the fifteen foot room.

"Have a seat and make yourself comfortable, Holly. You two also," she said looking at Bill and Kirk. I will finish getting dinner on and the doctor should be here within the hour."

Mrs. Morrison disappeared into the kitchen. Holly made sure that Jack's monitors were plugged in and working, and then checked him to make sure that he was okay. She sat down with a deep sigh.

"You don't need to be so nervous," Bill said.

"What makes you think that I am nervous?"

Bill looked at Kirk and they both smiled.

Looking back at Holly he said, "Let's just say I have a sense for that sort of thing."

Holly tried to relax, but she was in a strange house with people that she really didn't know, and she was not only responsible for her own safety, but for her son's safety also. She started to wonder about the wisdom of all of this. She sat quietly staring out the window watching the day grow darker and stormier looking. There was a bright flash, followed shortly by a loud crack of thunder that startled Holly. She quickly looked to make sure that Jack's machines didn't get turned off by a surge. They were okay. Suddenly, Holly could hear the steady down pour of rain on the roof of the little farm house.

"Well, I wouldn't want to be one of those troopers out on the highway in this," said Bill.

Holly looked out the window at the rain falling down and making everything outside shiny and wet. She felt cozy now, in the little house with the pot belly stove, and her worries began to melt away.

"Come and get it," said Mrs. Morrison from the doorway leading into the dining room.

Holly checked on Jack again, and then followed Bill and Kirk into the dining room. It was another large room with an old but beautiful table in the center. Along the far wall, next to the door leading to the kitchen, was a large hutch that held beautiful china. There was a large window at one end of the room through which Holly could see a well-manicured lawn surrounded by poplar trees. The table was set for five and the food looked and smelled delicious. Holly figured that the fifth place setting must be for the doctor. She supposed that the doctor was Marge's husband. After they sat down, Kirk reached out to take a roll, and his hand was quickly smacked away by Marge.

"Not until we give thanks" she said in a scolding tone.

Bill snickered and Holly couldn't help but smile at that. Marge closed her eyes and folded her hands together. The others followed her lead.

"Lord, we give thanks for this meal which we are about to receive. We ask thy blessing upon it. We pray that the doctor will arrive home safely, and ask thee to bless all those who are traveling to freedom this day. We are grateful to have Holly, Jack, Bill and Kirk with us, and pray for their continued safety as they travel. Amen."

Holly couldn't help but be touched by the thoughtful and sincere prayer from her hostess.

"Now," said Marge, "If you will hand me your plates, I will dish them up for you."

Kirk stuck his plate out, and Marge looked at him with a scowl.

"Ladies first," she said reaching for Holly's plate, "Good Lord! Where did you learn your manners?"

Truth be told, Kirk was very lacking in social graces. He was a large muscular man with tattoos on both arms. His head was shaved, and he seemed to always have a three day beard. Marge filled Holly's plate with roast, potatoes, broccoli and corn. As she handed Holly her plate back, she pointed to the gravy boat, and said, "Help yourself to some gravy dear, and have a roll with butter." While dishing up the other plates, Marge asked Bill to tell everybody a bit about themselves.

Bill was cleaner cut than Kirk. He looked like a Mormon bishop, with his well-groomed hair and nicely starched button down collar shirt with only the very top button undone. He explained that he had a wife and daughter at home. His wife had opened his eyes up to the terrible loss of freedom that they had suffered and together they actually sought out the CTDG. His daughter was born into a free family.

"So your daughter has never had any vaccines?" asked Holly.

"No, she has had one vaccine," he replied.

"I don't understand." said Holly, "I thought that the whole idea behind the CTDG was to not get vaccines or be implanted."

"Not at all," a man's voice from the doorway said. They all turned to see a young, dark haired man standing in the doorway from the kitchen. "Oh! It's the doctor" exclaimed Marge. "Come and sit down dear, I will get you a plate."

Holly thought that this man was much too young to be Marge's husband.

"Everybody, this is Dr. Craig Morrison, my son," said Marge. He reached around shaking hands with everybody before sitting down. Marge gave him each person's name as he shook their hand.

"In the other room, we have Holly's son Jack," Marge said.

Dr. Morrison sat down.

"The whole idea behind the CTDG is freedom," he said. "We need to have the biostrip in order to get along in the world, but we have been able to alter the biostrip to transmit and receive information that we want transmitted and received. We also want people to be free to pick and choose what, if any, vaccine they want."

"That is why," Bill spoke up, "We had our daughter receive the HIB vaccine when she was a baby. But that is the only vaccine that she has ever had."

Holly asked, "How then, does she go to school, and how can you afford all of this time off of work to take my son and I across the country?"

Doctor Morrison answered her, "The biostrip that we implant transmits up-to-date vaccine records for every one of us. It also carries all of the ICC that we need. We have a huge network of individuals with skills that the organization needs to help people be free. I regularly treat members of the CTDG as well as people who are still in bondage. Kirk here is a soldier for CTDG, and spends all of his time fighting for our cause. Bill is a transporter, and while he does have a job as a freelance consultant, he plays a big role in relocating people."

"So tell us about how you got involved," Holly said to Kirk.

"Well, I was raised in an orphanage, and set out on my own at the age of eighteen. I spent fifteen years in the Marines. I was married to the girl of my dreams. Her name was Tammy. We had a son, his name was Thomas, and he only lived four days."

Holly sat her fork down and listened intently as she realized that this was not going to be a happy story.

"My wife could not stand the pain that she felt over the loss of our son, so two weeks after he died, my wife took her own life. I had lost everything. So when someone from the "Connect the Dots Group" (CTDG) approached me, and told me about the opportunity of getting free, I was happy to join the cause and devote all of my time and skills to getting people out of bondage." There was a long silence at the table as everybody tried to take in his tragic story.

"Would you like some more roast?" asked Marge to Kirk, now in a softer and kinder tone.

"No, thank you," he said. "I need to go out and check the vehicle."

"In the rain?" asked Holly.

He didn't reply, but just got up and walked out. Marge didn't say anything about not asking to be excused, which she normally would have.

Dr. Morrison broke the silence after a few minutes, "So, Holly, you no doubt have questions about the procedure that we will be performing on you and your son early in the morning."

"Yes" said Holly, "I wasn't aware that there was going to be a procedure."

"Well", Dr. Morrison began, "We need to remove your current biostrips, and replace them with new ones that will in essence change your identities. You will then be able to travel anywhere that you need to undetected. Your new biostrip will also give you an unlimited amount of ICC's, and will also change your identity based on what region of the world you are in. Once you have decided on a permanent location, you can then lock in your identity. You also need to know that this new biostrip will communicate with you by stimulating the auditory and speech parts of your brain. When you think to yourself, 'Who am I,' you will hear the answer in your head. When you look at someone who has one of these new biostrips implanted, you will hear their name in your head. This way you will know who you can trust. You will also be able to pick up on other people's feelings and emotions."

Holly looked over at Bill who smiled and winked at her.

"Why are we waiting until tomorrow morning?" Holly asked.

"Because you just ate," the doctor replied. "We need to wait at least twelve hours before administering any anesthesia."

"So I will be asleep during the procedure?" asked Holly.

"Yes, but not for long. The procedure is fairly quick and recovery takes less than fifteen minutes. We will do Jack's first and allow you to observe."

Holly spent the rest of the evening sleeping in a recliner next to Jack, taking care of Jack, and wondering about Allen. At 1:30 A.M., Holly woke up and found Kirk sitting by Jack, holding his hand.

"What are you doing?" she asked.

"I just thought that I could watch him for a while and let you sleep. I know that this can be hard to do by yourself."

Holly was awe struck. She was seeing a tender side of Kirk that she didn't think he had. He had always seemed so mechanical and cold.

"Thank you," she said. "Do you know how to suction if you need to?"

"I have been watching you," he replied. "I think that I have got it. If I need help, I can wake you."

Holly looked at Jack, who was sound asleep, and then looked at Kirk who was looking at Jack's monitors. With gratitude, Holly got up out of the recliner and moved to a sofa where she could stretch out and sleep.

At about 4:30 the next morning, Marge came to Holly and said, "It is time. The doctor is ready to begin."

Holly got up, feeling more rested than she can ever remember feeling and with that, Kirk pushed Jack's bed to a room at the back of the house that had been converted to a surgical suite. She was given a stool to sit on at the foot of the surgical table and she watched as Kirk, Bill, Marge and Dr. Morrison carefully moved Jack to the surgery table and put him in a face down position. Marge went to the side of the table and began putting a pic line in Jack's arm.

She looked over at Holly and said, "Don't worry, I'm a certified nurse anesthetist."

This took Holly by surprise. Within a few moments they had Jack under and a sterile shield placed around the back of his head and neck. They then sterilized the area and began the surgical procedure.

"Before I make my first cut", Dr. Morrison said, "Are you squeamish at all?"

"Not anymore," Holly said. "I have seen Jack stuck, probed, prodded, and even cut many times. I can handle it."

Dr. Morrison made a small incision just at the base of Jack's hairline and opened the area up. He then took a long cotton swab and dipped it into a clear liquid and wiped it on the surface of Jack's skin around the incised area. Then he waited. Within a minute, Holly saw what looked like a black slug, with what looked like pinchers on its hind end, and what looked like a cobalt blue light pulsing down its back just under its flesh come slithering out of the hole in Jack's neck. She started to feel sick.

"What in the *hell* is that?!" Holly said loudly.

"That is the part of the biostrip system that the government doesn't want you to know about. It is called a 'host transmitter' or HT for short. Without it your biostrip would not work."

Dr. Morrison picked up the HT with a pair of surgical clamps and placed it in a jar. He then cleaned off the skin around the hole in the back of Jack's neck, and pulled some of the clear liquid that he had dabbed on there into a syringe. He then squirted a small amount of that liquid into the incision, as deep as he could get it.

"What is that stuff?" Holly asked.

"That is a pheromone. It attracts the HT into the site you want it to attach."

He took another surgical clamp and picked up a different slug looking creature and placed it just inside the hole. It quickly disappeared deep into the hole. Dr. Morrison then went to work closing the incision. After that incision was closed, Dr. Morrison sat down at the head of the table, and placed Jack's left hand on a hand rest by his head, palm down. He made a small, one half inch, incision on the back of his wrist just at the crease created when his hand bends back. He then pulled out a pair of clamps, and reached into the incision and pulled out a quarter inch by three quarter inch strip of what looked like plastic with circuits on one side.

"Now, that is what I thought was the biostrip," Holly said.

"That *is* the biostrip," said the doctor, "But this part only gathers information from the body, and stores it as well as personal information and ICC transactions.

Without the HT, this would just be an external memory with no way to access it unless it is removed."

"Doesn't it need batteries?" she asked.

"Nope. It picks up electrical energy from the body."

He then picked up a clean biostrip from a tray next to him and slid it into Jack's wrist. He gave him a few stitches there, and had Marge finish dressing his incisions and bringing him out of his anesthesia-induced nap. He escorted Holly out of the room and into the hallway.

"Let's wait until Jack is completely awake and then you can check on him and see to his needs before we do your procedure."

"Thank you," she said.

Within twenty minutes, Jack was awake and back in his own bed. Holly changed his diaper, and cleaned him up. She double checked his monitors and made sure that he was comfortable.

"I'm ready" she said.

She went into the operating room and lied down on the table. Before she knew it, she was waking up in the recovery room.

"Wow! That was quick."

Marge turned around from some work that she was doing across the room and said, "Welcome back Mrs. Trautner."

Holly hesitated for a moment, then asked, "What did you call me?"

"Mrs. Trautner, Beth Trautner. That is your name isn't it?" Marge asked.

Holly remembered what she had been told about her new biostrip, and she thought to herself, *Who am I?* and she heard her own voice in her head say, "Beth Trautner."

"Yes!" she said to Marge, "That is my name."

After twenty minutes and some juice, Beth got up and went to check on her son. As soon as she saw him, she heard her own voice in her head say, "Todd Trautner."

She smiled to herself as she checked his breathing and tubes and monitors. Kirk walked into the room.

"Are you ready to go?" he asked.

"Go where?" she replied.

"We need to get on the road and head for Indianapolis. We are supposed to meet some people there at the airport."

"Do you think that we are safe traveling in the van still? I know that we have new identities, but won't my son and the three of us fit a physical description?"

"You are right," said Kirk. "That's why you and Bill are traveling in the motor home with your son in a hidden room. I will be following in a light blue sedan."

CHAPTER 15

"**H**ENRY, I HAVE to get back to the medical center. I need to be there when she arrives," Dr. Calvin said.

"Right," said Henry.

They shook hands and went separate directions. Henry and James walked outside and went across the street to Temple Square. They crossed Temple Square and then crossed North Temple Street to the large conference hall. They entered the conference hall and took an elevator to the parking garage. Henry pulled his cell phone out and looked something up on it.

"Q37," he said to James.

They looked at the pillars to orient themselves, and then found Q37. In it was a Silver Cadillac. Henry pulled out a key and unlocked it. They got in and drove out of the parking structure toward the airport. Before getting to the airport, they pulled off in the park and wait area. Henry put the car in park and then pulled out his cell phone.

"I need to reset our identities before we enter the airport," he said to James.

Henry logged onto a secure site with his cell phone and pulled up James' account. He clicked on a search for ID button, and a second later there was a new ID information sheet on the screen.

"How would you like to live in Texas?" he asked James.

"What part of Texas?" James said.

"Fredericksburg," said Henry. "It is a small town northeast of San Antonio, population about twenty thousand."

"That sounds great!" James said.

Henry hit the accept button on the screen and after about thirty seconds, a box opened up that read *download successful.* Henry looked over at James and he heard his own voice in his head. Henry looked over at James and he heard his own voice in his head say, "Chris Fonsbeck."

"Hello Chris," said Henry.

James, now Chris, smiled. Next Henry pulled up his own profile, and again he clicked on *search ID*. A new ID came up.

He said, "Hilton Head Island, South Carolina. That sounds nice."

He hit the accept button and the progress wheel started to turn. Again, about thirty seconds later, a success window popped up. He asked himself in his mind, *Who am I?* He heard his own voice answer back in his head, "Joshua Labeaux".

"Do you go by Josh or Joshua?" asked James.

"I believe that I prefer Joshua," Henry answered.

He started the car and they drove to the long-term parking structure. He didn't have to worry about being scanned, because he now had a new identity. They took a few minutes to wipe the car clean of prints. Henry opened the trunk and each of them took out a small carry on suitcase. Each suitcase had a sticker on it with a number.

"I believe that mine was number 1," said Henry.

James looked at the sticker on his that had a number "1" on it.

Handing it to Henry he said, "Right."

They traded bags and then they entered the terminal.

"I need to go to Cheyenne to help our friends there. You should go home to Texas and get yourself settled," Henry said. "I think that I will go with United and I'm pretty sure that Delta goes to Texas."

They shook hands and gave each other a hug then went their separate ways to get tickets for their flights. Henry went up to an automated kiosk and scanned his wrist. His new name came up on the screen with the question, "Where are you going?" next to it. He started to type in Cheyenne, and after just getting the first three letters in a list of possible destinations came up. He chose Cheyenne, Wyoming, and then it gave him a list of departure times. He checked his watch. It was 10:45 A.M., and there was a flight leaving at 1:15 P.M.. He chose that flight. It then asked him what class he desired. He chose first class. The total ICC that would be deducted from his account popped up on the screen, 2500icc, and it asked him to approve that. He clicked approve. It then asked if he needed to check any baggage, to which he answered no. The word *Processing* appeared on the screen and flashed bright and dim slowly. After about fifteen seconds, the words *Processing Complete* appeared, followed by the words, *Proceed to gate A7*. He turned from the kiosk and walked to the security checkpoint. As he approached the scanners, a TSA guard approached him with a wand and asked to scan his wrist. She waved the wand over his wrist, and then looked at the read out on her wand.

"Are you going to Cheyenne on business or pleasure, Mr. Labeaux?" she asked.

"I am going to visit some friends," he answered with a kindly smile.

She smiled back and said, "You may use the green entry to your left, Mr. Labeaux. Have a nice trip."

Henry looked over at the short line at the green entry where people who had been through extensive background checks were allowed to walk through a body scanner without having to remove their belts and shoes. Carry-on luggage still had to go through an x-ray, but they did not have to remove electronics from their bags. The process was much faster. As he was picking up his bag on the inside of the security checkpoint, he looked over at the other entry and noticed the long line of people taking off items of clothing and putting electronics in trays. He began walking toward his gate, and then he noticed TSA personnel hurrying to each gate and setting up bio scanning stations. He wondered if they were looking for him already. He stopped at a small food vendor to buy a sandwich and a bottle of water. He noticed a TSA guard standing by the bioscanner where he would be paying for his food. He got a lump in his throat and butterflies in his stomach. *Well, here goes nothing*, he thought to himself. He waved his wrist over the scanner and looked at the guard.

"You don't have to worry, Mr. Labeaux," the guard said, obviously detecting an elevated heart rate in Henry. "There is no danger, we are just looking for someone."

"Thank God," said Henry.

He smiled and walked away with his food.

Well, they must be looking for Laura and Joel he thought, not realizing that it was him they were looking for. *I hope that they make it to Evanston alright.* He looked at his watch,.*11:15*, he thought to himself, *They should be well on their way to Evanston, already.* Then he thought about Eric. *If all went as planned, he should be downstairs right now renting his car.* Henry sat back and ate his sandwich slowly while waiting for the boarding call for his flight. After finishing his sandwich, he sat back to review what was going on with everyone. It had been quite an eventful day, and he was glad that he had made plans for just such a day. *I'm ready to be done after this,* he thought to himself.

Henry's mind turned to Holly. He walked to a quiet corner of the terminal, and took out his cell and made a call.

A woman answered, "Dr. Morrison's residence."

"Hello, this is Henry," he said. "I want to make sure that our friends are okay. Has there been any development?"

The woman responded, "They have put up road blocks on most of the main highways leaving the state, but we have people in position on their routes. We have told them to stay the course."

"Excellent," Henry replied, "Got to go."

Then Henry hung up the phone. He then placed another call.

A man answered, "This is Doug."

"Doug, this is Henry," he said. "I am going to patch a call through to your guest. Would you be so kind as to connect her phone for me please?"

"Of course, Henry," Doug said.

Then Henry put that call on hold and called Eric.

"Hello?" Eric said.

"Eric, this is Henry. I am going to connect you with Sarah for a quick minute so that you can put her mind at ease a bit. Hold just a second."

After connecting the call, Henry allowed them to talk for about twenty seconds, then he disconnected the call. *I'll explain everything to Eric when I talk with him in about forty-five minutes,* Henry thought to himself. Henry sat back and took inventory. *I have Holly with Kirk and Bill; they are doing well. I have Eric on his way to meet his family in Evanston, and he has already received a new biostrip. James is on his way to Texas, and I am here. By this time tomorrow night, we should all be sitting around a warm fire in my cabin.*

CHAPTER 16

HOLLY AND BILL loaded Jack into the motorhome and made sure that he was secure. They had the motorhome set up so that Holly could be right by Jack the whole time, and if they were approaching a road block they could conceal Jack.

"Won't they be able to detect Jack's biostrip?" Holly asked Bill as they started down the highway.

"Yes, but his name will not be Jack Cranfield, and we can just tell them that he is asleep."

They made it all the way to Pittsburgh before they had to stop for gas and some food. Having the motorhome was a real advantage. Holly was very surprised that they hadn't seen any road blocks the entire way. She had also been worried about Jack. She was sure that he had a headache from the surgery, because she did. He had acted a bit agitated and she was unable to give him anything for his headache. She had been able to control hers with some Tylenol.

"I wonder why we haven't seen any road blocks," Holly said.

"I think that once we got a little outside the state of Maryland, it becomes pretty difficult to block all of the possible routes that we could be taking. I'm sure that they will be doing random checks and the circle that they are searching in will continue to grow." Bill answered. "After we stop and fill up the gas tank, and get some dinner, do you think that you could drive for a bit while I get some sleep? You should be able to hear Jack's alarms if something goes wrong and you could just pull over. Or we could just stop for a few hours while I sleep."

Holly thought for a minute then replied, "I feel so bad that I am taking you away from your family like this. Your wife must be worried sick. I don't mind driving for a while, that way we can get to where we are going sooner and get you back to your family sooner."

After filling up the gas tank, they stopped at a McDonald's for food. Bill positioned the motorhome across the street from the McDonald's in a dark area with the back of the motorhome toward McDonald's. Holly stayed in the motorhomewhile Bill went in for the food. Holly waited for what seemed like thirty minutes, then she decided to see what was taking so long. She couldn't leave Jack, but she could just walk around to the back of the motorhome and see if she could see Bill in the restaurant. As Holly walked around the back of the motorhome, her heart sank, and she began to breathe rapidly as she saw three police cars in the parking lot of the McDonald's with their lights on. She saw somebody sitting in the back of one of the police cars, but all she could see was a silhouette. Just then she heard a phone ringing inside the motor home. She ran inside and searched frantically for the phone. She found it in a pocket on the side of the driver's seat after about six rings.

"Hello, hello?"

"Holly?" a familiar woman's voice said.

"Yes, this is Holly, who is this?"

"Mrs. Morrison, are you okay?"

"Oh!" Holly said with a sigh of relief. "Am I glad to hear your voice! I don't know where Bill is, he went into a McDonald's to get us some food and that was a half an hour ago. Now there are police cars all around the McDonald's and Bill is nowhere to be seen. What should I do?" Holly was not panicking, but she was close to tears.

"That is why I called," said Mrs. Morrison. "We received word that Bill had been apprehended in the McDonald's. Somebody recognized a picture of him that had been on the news."

"How did they know to be looking for him?" Holly asked.

"We don't know for sure, but we think that maybe they picked up some surveillance video of him either outside your apartment or at the mall or something.They don't know who he really is, though, because he changes his biostrip identity when he is on these missions. That way his family is safe."

"What happens to him now?" Holly asked.

"We are not sure, but we do know that Henry has people on the inside that might be able to help Bill. That is what we are hoping for."

Holly was hopeful also.

"So should I just continue traveling?" Holly asked.

"NO. You can't travel alone with your son, so we will get some help to you. Kirk is out there, he just wants to make sure that the coast is clear before coming to the motorhome. You should just stay with the motorhome and wait. There is a gun in the glove compartment. Do you know how to use one?"

Holly swallowed deep and replied, "Uh yeah, I think so. It has been a while, but I used to go shooting with my Dad."

"Good," Mrs. Morrison said. "I don't think that you will need it, but have it handy just in case. Consider yourself at war, and you are trapped behind enemy lines. Lie low and be prepared. Kirk will be there before dawn."

The phone went dead. Holly put down the phone, and felt very alone. She was in a strange place, with her severely handicapped son and she was being looked for by the police. She had never been this afraid. Holly opened the glove compartment and took out the gun. It was a black 45 caliber pistol. She thought back to her childhood, and shooting a pistol just like this with her Dad before they were outlawed. She thought how she was now breaking another law by being in possession of a gun. Guns were still pretty prevalent even though they had been outlawed. She looked over the gun and became re-acquainted with it by identifying the different parts. She popped out the ten round clip and found it to be full. She was startled back to her present situation when she was suddenly illuminated by bright lights from a car just to the left and behind her a bit. She quickly popped the magazine back into the gun, and locked in a round. After taking off the safety, she slowly and carefully looked over her left shoulder to see a police car just thirty feet away. She wondered what she would do. *Could she shoot another human being, let alone a policeman?* She was sick at the thought, but she also knew that she could not allow herself to be taken in, as that would mean never seeing her son again. Her heart was pounding and her hands were shaking as she saw the policeman get out of his car and start to approach the motorhome. He stopped about ten feet away, still slightly toward the rear of the motorhome and gestured for her to roll her window down. She held the gun with her right hand hanging down at her side and with her left hand rolled her window down.

"Ma'am, I need to ask you to step out of the vehicle."

Just then she heard a muffled crack followed by a thud, and she saw the officer's head explode as he dropped to the ground. She dropped her gun and instantly began vomiting. As soon as she finished heaving, Kirk was opening the door of the motorhome and telling her that she had to quickly move her son to an ambulance that was parked on the right side of the motorhome. Holly was in shock. Everything seemed to move in slow motion, and sounds were muffled and distant. It was almost as if she were an outside observer watching herself do the things that she needed to do. While she moved Jack, Kirk quickly put the officer in his car and drove in down into a wooded ravine just in front of the motorhome. He came back to the ambulance and got into the driver's seat.

"Are you okay?" he asked Holly.

Holly was lethargic and pale. She looked at Kirk for quite a while before giving him a faint nod. Kirk turned on the lights and siren, and drove quickly away. After about five minutes, Holly was able to speak.

"Where are we going?" she asked.

"To a small airstrip," he replied. "We have a private jet waiting for us."

Within fifteen minutes, they were in the jet and taxiing for take off. Once they were airborne, Holly felt like she could breathe again. She checked on Jack, then looked over at Kirk who was sitting quietly in his chair watching her care for Jack. Holly looked up at Kirk, and wondered about the man that was so tender and caring just last night, and then minutes ago blew a man's head open. She knew that Allen was capable of that kind of violence, but he was not capable of the tenderness. She could not reconcile that.

Holly moved to the chair next to Kirk and asked, "What just happened Kirk?"

"We are at war," he replied.

"That means that sometimes we have to kill. There really was no other way to avoid you getting caught."

Holly nodded then sat back. She was grateful to be safe with Kirk, and she felt safe and secure for the first time in years, even though she was on the run. Her thoughts then turned to the policeman, and quietly wept as she thought of that poor officer's family.

CHAPTER 17

ERIC PULLED INTO the parking lot of the McDonald's, and parked to the side of the motor home. He was hoping that this was the right one. Henry had given him a description, but he still was a bit apprehensive. He turned off his car and sat there for a moment trying to plan his strategy. He remembered that if they were with Henry's group, then as soon as he was within a few yards of them he would hear a name in his head. *How many yards?* He couldn't remember. *Do I have to see them?* he wondered. He was hoping that he could just walk up to the side of the motorhome and hear a name without knocking on the door first. He walked over to the motor home and just stood by the left side of it for a moment concentrating and trying to hear a name. *Nothing*, he thought. He decided that he would go ahead and knock on the door and if he didn't hear a name, he would just say that he made a mistake. This was very difficult for Eric. He hated looking like an idiot. He walked around to the right side of the motor home and knocked on the side door. He heard some people walking around inside, and some muffled voices. After about thirty seconds, the door opened and he saw Clare standing there in front of him. At the same time, he heard her name, Clare Homer, in his head.

"Eric!" Clare exclaimed with relief in her voice. "I was hoping that it was you."

Eric then noticed the barrel of a rifle that was aimed right at his head through the crack of the door slowly move down and away.

"I'm grateful that it is me, also," he said.

Clare let Eric in and as he stepped up into the motor home, he saw a man standing in the kitchen area with a rifle down to his side. "Doug Homer," he heard in his head. Doug reached out to shake hands with Eric.

"Good to meet you, Eric," he said even though he heard the name "Tom Chandler" in his head.

"Nice to meet you also, Doug," Eric said. "I don't want to be rude, but I'm very anxious to see my wife and son."

Clare, who was standing there just smiling at Eric from ear to ear, suddenly jerked back into the moment and said, "OH! Of course you are. I'm sorry. Laura and Eric, Jr. are just inside that room. You go ahead and go in, we will get moving."

"Thank you" Eric said as he walked through the kitchen to the door she had pointed at.

As Eric opened the door he felt like he had passed through some type of teleportation device that was connected to the hospital. He couldn't believe how much bit looked like a hospital room inside. Laura was sitting in a rocking chair, with her back to the door. She was nursing Eric, Jr. Eric walked up behind her and looked down at his wife and son. He didn't say anything for a few seconds, but when she started to turn her head to the left to see who had come in, he thought that he better say something.

"Hi, honey," he said.

He was surprised by Laura's reaction. She didn't look up, or stop nursing, she just started to weep. Eric quickly came around to the front of her chair and dropped down on one knee.

"I'm so sorry, Laura. I didn't mean to scare you or put you through any of this, but it was somewhat out of my hands."

He put his arms around her gently and gave her a kiss. Then he gently wiped the tears away from her eyes. They felt the motorhome begin to move. Sarah noticed something different about Eric. He seemed more present than he had ever seen before.

"Eric," she said, "What is going to happen now?"

Eric looked down and thought for a minute how he could explain things to her.

"Laura," he said, "I have made a decision that will change our lives forever. I have had my government biostrip removed, and have had a new one inserted. My name isn't even Eric Dunn anymore, it is Tom Chandler."

Laura looked at Eric as her heart raced. She wondered for a moment how she should react. Her initial impulse was to be angry. She didn't follow her initial impulse, she waited momentarily, and thought it through. If she got angry and left Eric, she would never see him again, and Eric, Jr. would never know his Dad. She remembered what that meant to her in her life, and she couldn't bear the thought of that. On the other hand, if she didn't get angry and leave him then she would have to have her bioscan changed and they would have to start a life somewhere else as different people. On the plus side, she would have her mother in her life, but Eric would not have his parents in his life. *That would be a plus for me*, she thought to herself.

"Say something" he said to her.

"Well Mr. Chandler" she said, "Tell me, do you have a wife? And if not, do you want one?"

Eric breathed out a deep breath of relief.

"I love you so much," he said. "Will you be my wife?"

Sarah smiled, "On one condition," she said. "Don't ever scare me like that again."

Eric kissed her passionately, "I promise," he said, and then kissed her again. The motorhome stopped moving and there was a knock on the door.

"Come in," Eric said.

Clare opened the door and stepped in.

"Eric" Laura said, "I want to introduce you to my Mom and your mother–in-law, Rose Brady, also known as Clare Homer."

Eric looked at Laura with a surprised look on his face, "Do you mean that Clare is your real Mom?"

"That is exactly what I mean."

Eric looked at Clare, "Why didn't you tell me?"

"I didn't think that it was safe to tell you yet," she replied.

Eric just stood there taking it all in for a moment.

"And Doug?"

"He is my husband, and that makes him your father-in-law."

"Well," Eric said, "I guess that it is normal for my first meeting with my father-in-law to include him pointing a rifle at me."

They all laughed.

Clare said, "We are at the safe house. We will stay here tonight, and tomorrow morning Laura and Eric, Jr. will receive their new biostrips. Then we will travel to Cheyenne to meet up with Henry."

They walked out of the motorhome and Laura looked around. They were in a nice little neighborhood, with clean modest homes. The house that they were entering was a white brick home with a two-car garage and a clean, well-kept yard. They entered the house and it was a split level entry. Laura thought how the house had a pleasant "Grandma and Grandpa" like feel to it. They followed Clare and Doug up the stairs to the main floor. At the top of the stairs, Clare led them down a hallway to the right. They passed a bathroom on the left, and two bedrooms on the right. At the end of the hallway was the master bedroom.

"You guys will sleep in here," she said.

The master bedroom had a large bed in it with a small bassinet on a stand in the corner of the room.

"Now get settled in, and I will go to the kitchen and make some dinner."

"I can help you," Laura said.

"No," said Clare, "You two have some things to talk about, like where do you want to live? What do you want to do? There is a TV in the living room if you want to relax for a bit."

Clare left the room and went into the kitchen. Doug went outside to clean and close up the motorhome.

"So what now?" said Laura.

"Well, I guess we need to make some decisions, like Clare said," replied Eric.

They spent the next hour talking. Eric told Laura about the biostrip surgery, and all of his activities with Henry. They discussed what they wanted to do with their lives from that point on, and at the end of the hour, had decided that they wanted to live somewhere in the western United States and wanted to help others get free.

"Dinner is ready," Clare called down the hallway.

They went to the kitchen and found a nice, homemade chili and cornbread dinner waiting for them. They had a pleasant meal together and spent a couple of hours at the table just talking and catching up. Laura felt at home, and was grateful to be with her Mom. Eric really enjoyed talking with Doug, who was very computer savvy.

Clare said, "So tomorrow morning, the doctor will be here to do the biostrip implants. We will do Eric, Jr. first, and you can both observe. Then we will do Laura. Do you have any questions about the procedure, Laura?" asked Clare.

"No, Eric has filled me in."

Laura went to the bedroom to feed Eric, Jr. and Eric helped Doug and Clare clean up dinner. Lying in bed that night, Eric couldn't believe how alive and free he felt. Early the next morning they were awoken by Clare.

"The doctor is here, and we are ready to proceed."

Clare led them downstairs where there was a surgical suite set up. Laura watched as the doctor and Clare carefully prepped and performed the procedure that Eric had described to her on their little baby boy. It was quick and simple, and Eric, Jr only cried when they gave him a local anesthetic shot. She and Eric took Eric, Jr. upstairs and made sure that he was comfortable.

"I will stay up here with Eric, Jr. while you get yours done," Eric said. Laura agreed, and headed downstairs. She remembered lying down on the table face down and then waking up in a recovery bed an hour later.

"You stayed out a bit longer than usual," Clare said when she noticed that Laura was awake. "I guess you were a bit worn out after all the excitement over the last few days."

"Are we all done?" Laura asked.

"Yes we are Mrs. Chandler," Clare said with a wink and a grin.

Laura had some mild localized pain in her wrist and the back of her head, but other than that she felt fine. They went upstairs and found Eric sitting in the living room with Doug, who was holding Eric, Jr. Eric stood up as they entered the room.

"How do you feel?" he asked Laura.

"Fine," she said.

"Well," Doug said, "The cars are loaded and ready to go. We should get going to Cheyenne." "Cars?" asked Laura.

"Yes," said Clare, "We will be traveling in two separate cars, caravan style."

"If we leave now, and stop once for lunch, we can be there by four o'clock this afternoon," Doug said.

CHAPTER 18

ONE DAY AFTER arriving, Director Alice Henderson sat at on the sofa in her hotel room at the Grand America Hotel in Salt Lake City, Utah wondering how she could have possibly lost so many suspects of bioterrorism in just three days. She had just got off the telephone with the Homeland Security office in Pennsylvania. They had informed her of a police officer that had been shot, and they suspected that it had something to do with one of the terrorists that they had apprehended earlier that evening. They then informed her that the suspect that they had apprehended had somehow just disappeared.

I don't get it! I did everything right, she thought to herself. *We checked surveillance video, we tracked biostrip scanners, and we had road blocks and even put out pictures on TV. So how did ten people just up and disappear, especially when we had one of them in custody?* She realized then that the only person that they had taken into custody was because of pictures put out through the media and not because of the biostrip scans.

"They are somehow manipulating the bioscanners," she said to herself out loud. *Why is it that we could not pick up any cell phone or internet chatter on any of this activity?* she wondered. Just then her cell phone rang.

"Director Henderson," she said after pushing the talk button on her phone.

"Director, this is a secure call, please authenticate," a female voice said.

The director took her key fob out of her pocket and pushed the button. "Authentication, Black Bird," she said.

"I will connect your call," the woman on the other end of the phone line said.

After a short pause, she heard a man with a British accent speaking to her.

"Director, you do not know who I am, but I represent the One World Alliance of the United Nations and we need your full cooperation."

Director Henderson's heart began to beat more rapidly.

"I'm sorry, but you are right, I don't know who you are, but I do not work for anyone other than the President of the United States, and the people of the United States."

"Director?" she heard a familiar female voice.

"This is President Clifton. I need you to cooperate with these people. They will tell you what you need to know, and then you will need to act accordingly. We need to put a stop to this bioterrorist activity and without the information that they are going to give you, you will not be able to do your job."

"Yes, Madam President," the Director replied.

"Very well," said the man with the British accent, "We shall move on then. As I said, we are the *One World Alliance*, but you can call us *The System*.

"How many people make up *The System*?" she asked.

"It doesn't matter," he replied curtly. "I will tell you what you need to know to do your job, and no more. Asking questions will only make this conversation longer and much more tedious than it need be. You are an intelligent person, and therefore should understand what I tell you without the need for clarifying questions."

Director Henderson did not reply, but she did feel her face and neck getting hot as her anger and indignation grew.

"Very well," he said, "Let us continue. The leader of the terrorist cell you are chasing is Henry Cranfield. He is the inventor of the biostrip as we know it and use it now. When Henry first developed the biostrip, we saw it as a tool that could be implemented worldwide to do away with the need for currency and passports and also a way to make sure that people are getting their proper vaccines, and staying away from public places when they are ill, and so forth. It was a tool that we had looked for, for quite some time, to bring about our designs of a unified world. Henry did not like our ideas, and without our knowledge, he began developing a second type of biostrip that would not only integrate with our system, but it would also write to our system. Essentially, Dr. Cranfield is able to create and change identities for anyone who has one of his biostrips. This affords them unlimited amounts of ICC's, and the ability to move about the world undetected and un-vaccinated. This is why you have not been able to capture the terrorists. We have known about him for some time, but also knew that he had to have help on the inside. We did not want to move on him until we had found his mole. Through a complex sting operation that we have conducted inside the system, we were able to identify three key players in Dr. Cranfield's organization that were working inside the system. We did not make a move on them yet, but are ready to now. For the last year and a half, we have had a team working on a solution. We have developed now an algorithm that we can implement that will isolate all of Dr. Cranfield's counterfeit biostrips. We plan on taking care of the three infiltrators, and then implementing the new algorithm. When we do all of the people who have counterfeit biostrips will suddenly be without identity and without ICC's. You must understand Director, you have moles within your organization. When we flip the switch, it will be like turning on a light in a dark room full of cockroaches. You will see them start to scurry. We will not announce this to anyone, but will allow the people involved to sweat. It is time for them to know that *The System* giveth, and *The System* taketh away.

Edwards Brothers Malloy
Thorofare, NJ USA
May 9, 2014